THE

COURTS

ON MAPLE

DRIVE

THE COURTS ON MAPLE DRIVE

~A NOVEL~

GAIL BENICK

IGUANA

Publisher: Cheryl Hawley
Editor: Marie-Lynn Hammond
Front cover design: Ruth Dwight, designplayground.ca

ISBN 978-1-77180-708-1 (paperback)
ISBN 978-1-77180-707-4 (epub)

This is a work of fiction. Unless otherwise stated, all the names, characters,
places, events and incidents in this book are either the product of the author's
imagination or used in a fictitious manner. Any resemblance to actual persons,
living or dead, is purely coincidental.

This is an original print edition of *The Courts on Maple Drive*.

In loving memory of Les Benick
1940–2023
Brother, mentor, mensch

CHAPTER 1

Heidi

July 2023

Joanne K. has added the following note to the Pickleball session you signed up for at Maple Drive Park on Tuesday, July 11 @ 7:15PM: Running a bit late. See you around 7:30.

What the fuck? Don't know her or anything, but really. Whoever she is, can't she at least show up on time? Why else would you use the Pickleball Organizer if you can't be bothered to come when you're supposed to. There goes our first game down the shitter.

Almost no power left again on this dumb phone to contact the organizers. The battery is total crap. Who in the hell are Ron G. and Lisa M. anyway? He's rated here at 3.0 and she's at 3.25. Says who? These ratings don't mean a thing. No idea what my rating is, but when I signed up, I put in Heidi A. (2.5). Really, who cares? Let's just get on the court and play already.

What a complete shambles Maple Drive is. Nothing like when I grew up here. This street was the crème de la crème. Fancy-shmancy, with apple trees and a duck pond in the park across from our house. Mamaleh, my shrinking little mama, used to tell me, "Don't feed the ducks. Careful. One might bite off your finger." Now I see a plump, painted metal rooster figurine likely plucked from someone's dumpster sitting in the front garden at number 33. One person's trash is another person's treasure, as they say.

I would really like to know when the city is planning to move all these mammoth John Deeres off the road so I can cross the street to the park without beheading myself. Is that too much to ask? The sign says, "Please excuse the mess and the noise. We're installing new sewers to manage basement flooding." Thanks. It's about time. But the tractors are so loud during the day that Mamaleh can't have a decent nap. I guess that's why she's so damn cranky all the time. Never content. Buy some grapes, she orders me. Green only. That skirt's too short on you. Half of your you-know-what is sticking out. But when she said during a recent afternoon visit, "You'd rather go out looking like a tart with a stranger than staying here to have a tea with your own mother," I knew I had to put some distance between us. Her demands are over the top. Way too much for me. No matter how hard I try to slough them off, she tries to keep me close by pulling on an invisible chain that brings me back into her space whenever I try to occupy my own. And her orders never end. Today it's a cup of tea and a new mattress for her bed. Tomorrow she'll want me to move back in. No fucking way.

At the end of last summer, I saw a work crew resurfacing the tennis courts in the park across from her house. But something was odd about the way they drew the boundary lines on the asphalt. When I stood by the edge of the fence, I noticed that the lines were different colours: some white and others yellow. The yellow lines defined a smaller surface area and were drawn inside the white boundary lines. Pretty confusing for my old brain, I'm ashamed to confess.

Then, about three weeks later—it must have been in early September—I crossed through the park on my way home and saw that nets were up. Four people were playing on one of the courts. Not tennis, though. Something else. Something played with a paddle, a bit bigger than the ping pong paddle that sits idle on the ping pong table in Mamaleh's basement. Nobody has played in decades.

"We've been pickled," I heard a player say.

"Yup. You didn't score a single point," another player gloated.

"Hey, what game are you playing?" I said as they walked off the court. I pushed my face close to the chain links while watching them drink from their water bottles.

"Pickleball," the guy closest to the fence said between slurps. He grinned.

"Are we on for tomorrow night?" a third person asked.

It all sounded silly to me. I couldn't believe that anyone would ever take seriously a game with a bizarre name like that. Yet there they were, having fun—a novel concept—and arranging to play again. Listening to them, I decided to try playing this pickle thing, not because I enjoy sports. I'm the biggest klutz in the universe and wouldn't typically consider joining any kind of competitive team. Not on your life. But if I started to play pickleball, I could tell Mamaleh I had a big date whenever she begged me not to leave. A date! She'd never argue with that. Pickleball, in the beginning, was the fastest way I could think of to gain a bit of separation from her. I was so desperate that I knew I had to make it work. And pickleball seemed to be a better way to find a partner than an online dating app where scammers lurk by the dozens.

Now, almost a year later, I cross Maple Drive and enter the park. The grass is still dewy from rain. My running shoes feel squishy and uncomfortable. A few kids hang upside down on the slick climber, and several boys slosh around in the mud. I guess the wet muck is good for making valleys and streams or digging for worms. Tyler, my youngest grandson, would love it here. It's easier to please him than my three grown-up sons, Josh, Ben, and Simon, who are always badgering me about something, like not driving after dark. What am I supposed to do? Sit home alone and knit potholders?

In the park, a baseball game is in progress not far from where the pond used to be. Most of the apple trees are gone too. Just a few clumps of evergreens remain in the far northwest corner, standing tall like hulking shadows in the early evening light, and a maple with spindly limbs that arc over the restroom nearby. If one of those branches happens to snap, it could kill someone.

I fiddle with the latch on the gate until it springs open, then enter. All three courts are full.

Nobody looks even vaguely familiar. The woman on the closest court wears black running shorts and a baseball cap. I feel ridiculous in my tennis skirt that reveals the varicose veins on the back of my upper legs, like pale purple Twizzlers. My sun visor doesn't hide the tufts of grey hair spiking from the top of my head. What was I thinking when I bought it? It must have been on the reduced rack at Winners.

The man next to the woman turns to me. "You're Heidi, right? I saw your name on the Pickleball Organizer." He looks to be sixty-something, a trim, sporty type with a slight accent that I can't identify. British? Australian? South African?

"Yup. That's me."

"I'm Ron. Nice to meet you."

The woman beside him says, "Hi. I'm Lisa. We're just waiting for Joanne." She glances across the park at two women chatting as they walk along the path to the courts.

"I hope you don't mind," Joanne says when they arrive. "I brought my friend Sylvia Greene. We can all rotate if that's okay with you guys."

I'm confused. Not only is Joanne late, but she expects each of us to give up a game so her friend can play, which totally sucks. Sylvia, a streaked blonde with a closed expression, barely smiles to acknowledge our generosity. She seems to keep her emotions under wraps, unlike me. I make no effort to disguise my irritation.

"Let's start already. What are we waiting for?"

The truth is, I hadn't planned to say a word tonight, but now that I have, I'm afraid that I've made a mistake inserting myself into this. Into this what, I wonder. Into the group? Into pickleball? But maybe I haven't made such a big mistake, because Ron seems to be looking at me attentively, as if he's assessing my winnability or my availability or, if I'm lucky, both.

"I'll play with you, Heidi," he says. "Against Lisa and Joanne. Sylvia can play in the next game."

I nod and pull down the brim of my visor to create a snug fit. One of those little habits that quiets my nerves and boosts my confidence for some unfathomable reason.

"Do you want to warm up?" Joanne asks. I'm ready to shriek from her endless procrastination. Maybe we should have a six-course meal before we begin too.

"I've played at the gym this morning and at Banbury in the afternoon," Lisa says, tossing the ball to Ron. "Just start. Your serve. 0-0-2."

Ron bounces the ball and smacks a serve to Lisa, who is playing back beyond the baseline. Her return comes at me, hard and fast. I miss it. Staring at the paddle in disbelief, I flip it over to see if there's a hole in the other side. Nope. This paddle is too fucking heavy for me. It must be made of teak and granite. The truth is, I stink at this. I can't even keep my wrist firm. Furious, I make a fist and punch the air.

"Shit," I say under my breath, rubbing my paddle hand up and down on my skirt to wipe off the perspiration. "Sorry, Ron."

"Next time," he says. "And forget the sorry."

Lisa announces the score—0-0-1—and serves to Ron, who sends the ball down the sideline to Joanne, who whacks the ball diagonally across the court to me. I miss it again. I stink under pressure. Lisa and Joanne draw close together and whisper something I can't hear.

"Watch out," Ron says. "They're going to target you."

"Huh? I'm a beginner. No fair." I'm praying to get through this game by putting at least one point on the board, and then I'll make up some excuse to take off.

"You're obviously the weakest player," Ron says. "They're forcing you to beat them. Smart."

Before I can respond, Lisa calls out the score, 1-0-1, and serves to me. For the third time, I miss the shot. Joanne shakes her head at my error. Ron shrugs. Lisa announces the new score: 2-0-1. The numbers scramble in my head. Who invented a scoring system where a series of three numbers constantly flip-flops? So complicated. I need *Pickleball for Dummies* to keep it all straight. There goes my concentration. Bye-bye game. I hate being a loser, but that's what I am. It feels like a scarlet *L* is taped to my forehead.

We gather at the centre of the court to touch paddles, but somehow it doesn't seem like a friendly closing gesture.

"How long have you been playing, Heidi?" Lisa is trying to sound interested without being overtly judgmental.

I look down at my feet, feeling guilty about wrecking their game. "About eight months. But I've also taken a few lessons so I'm not a newbie anymore. I just want to play as much as I can."

"Right," drawls Joanne, not even pretending to be empathetic.

"I love the pop sound when the ball hits the paddle," I enthuse for her benefit. "It makes me feel so alive."

Joanne turns away without responding.

I'm about to cry, well, almost cry. Shedding tears is not something women in my generation do in public. It makes us appear too fragile and dainty, like wearing a pink babydoll outfit. A definite no-no. Those stereotypes have to be crushed, totally. No sobbing, whining, or giving in permitted. That's how we intend to rewrite the story of not mattering.

Lisa Melman has organized a new session for doubles play B4 going away for 2 weeks at Maple Drive Park on Thursday, July 27 from 1:00 PM to 3:00 PM.

Please pay strict attention to the following note from Lisa: I urge you not to inflate your skill level to a 3.0 if it you are not actually at that level, just to get into this or any other session. Fair is fair.

Click here for further details and join us.

When I log in and open the schedule, I see that Ron and Sylvia have signed up to play with Lisa again, but Joanne's name is missing. That asshole. Does she think she's too good to play with them? They're solid intermediates at a 3.0 or above, so what's the problem? Frankly, Joanne is not nearly as good as she thinks she is. And who's this Andrew L. (3.5)? The last thing I want to deal with is a pumped-up egomaniac. Still, I press the Sign Me Up button. Done.

Andrew L., I discover when I meet him on the court, is a short, middle-aged man with poker-straight glossy black hair. He immediately tells me that he's an accomplished tennis player. No wonder he's wearing his tennis whites, though his shirt with a frayed collar has seen better days. So has my cutesy tennis skirt, which I've replaced today with black tights. Sylvia and I decide to take on Ron and Andrew. Girls against the boys. Big mistake. Andrew plays as if he's still playing tennis, rarely moving up to the kitchen line, the section in front of the net where you're not allowed to hit the ball before it touches the ground. Even I know that. When he bangs the ball at my feet for the third time, I succeed in scooping his low shot. Uh-oh. He returns my high ball with a smash down the middle. Neither Sylvia nor I get there in time to return it. We look at each other and shrug.

"No worries. Nothing we can do about it, right?" Sylvia is trying her best to reassure me. I'm grateful for any positive reinforcement she sends my way because playing against Andrew doesn't exactly spark joy. Her nonjudgmental attitude is exactly what I need. Then she adds, "Are you okay?"

"Sure. I'm fine. Thanks." I manage to smile. Trying to sound upbeat, I shout, "Great shot, Andrew. But I set you up for it."

He's deadpan. When he serves to me again, I don't even attempt to connect with the ball. Reaching into the thigh pocket of my tights, I pull out my vibrating phone and say hello.

"Hey, Heidi," Andrew calls out. "Tell the duct cleaner to call back later. You're either playing or get off the court. Lisa can play for you."

"It's my ninety-three-year-old mother," I yell back. "You want me to let her die, Andrew?"

He walks off the court, grumbling that we're wasting his time. Ron asks Lisa to take Andrew's place. I detect that he's pissed off too.

"Sorry for the disruption, Ron," Sylvia says, trying to de-escalate a potentially explosive situation. She seems to be good at it, as if there's a snug-fitting seal she's clamped onto her emotions. More power to her. But really, I don't get it. Why are women always apologizing when there's nothing to be sorry for? That's my eternal question.

"Can't you go somewhere else to play at your own level?" Andrew says. He stares directly at me as he departs.

I feel as small as an ant that he's rubbed out with the toe of his tennis shoe. On the phone, Mamaleh reminds me to get her some fresh grapes. "Not red ones. They're tasteless."

Give me a break just once, I'm tempted to tell her, so I can get my head inside pickleball and focus on playing a half-decent game.

About forty minutes later, an alert appears on the screen of my phone: Heavy rain expected in your area in the next three minutes. I look up at the bloated clouds hovering above. A clap of thunder forces us to pack up our paddles and court shoes.

"Let's go. Anyone need a lift home?" I ask.

"Me," Sylvia says.

"Run. I parked in my mother's driveway up the street."

Once in the car, Sylvia tells me she lives only a couple of blocks away. A few wisps of hair have come loose from her hairband. Otherwise, everything about Sylvia is perfectly controlled, from her hands folded in her lap to her foot tapping like a metronome against her oversized Lolë tote bag. I bet she has three pairs of the exact same respectable grey pants hanging in her closet, all in a row, and two more thin metal hairbands like the blue one she's wearing, but maybe—and it's a long shot—the other hairbands are in different colours.

"Are you still working?" I ask, trying to place her age. She looks younger than my seventy-three years, not that it matters. She has probably demonstrated a quiet maturity from the time she was a toddler.

"No, I'm retired," she says. "From an accounting firm. You?"

"I was a consultant in org development. Mostly public sector contracts. My own business, but that was then." I smile. "Now pickleball is my career."

"I may be wrong," Sylvia says, "but for me, pickleball is a form of exercise that should never become an obsession. We're not going to achieve a world ranking in our lifetimes, so why get stressed over how we play…don't you think? Honestly, who cares?"

I care passionately. In fact, I'd like my obituary to include a photo of me looking svelte, clutching an extraordinarily expensive pickleball paddle instead of the one I use now from Canadian Tire. But I'm embarrassed to tell Sylvia that because she'll think I'm wildly unrealistic, and she won't want to become friends. The last thing I need is one less supporter on the court. It's demeaning enough that the more advanced players scatter to other courts when I offer to join their game. It reminds me of being chosen second to last on the baseball team in high school. I still haven't forgotten standing near home plate with my lips quivering. *Please, please. Someone choose me!*

"It's the need to master something," I say after a few seconds. "I'm not competitive, but learning to do something I couldn't do before would be cool. I don't want to shrivel up and die just because I'm old when I still might have potential, right? Don't you want to improve?" A bolt of lightning flashes as the car crawls up to the top of the street.

"To be honest, I'm not all that driven by the need to improve," Sylvia says. "Pickleball is just a way to have fun. That's why I'm here—for the fun of it. But even a novice like me knows that unless you play with people who are better than you are, you'll never get better."

That's a message I'd prefer not to hear. I detest the thought of moving on and deserting the beginners I've connected with. Where I come from, loyalty is a virtue. It was drilled into us—me and my younger brother, Ian—from an early age. Mamaleh insisted that we stick together—take care of each other—and I usually did look after Ian because I'm five years older than he is, and he is my only sibling. But one time I left him in the park when he was a little boy. It happened on a summer day. I bumped into some of my pals on the climber. Ian sat building forts in the sandbox, perfectly content. "Let's go to my house for some lemonade," one of the girls said. All of them were going, so I left without telling Ian. I figured he wouldn't miss me, but he did. Someone saw him crying and asked where he lived, then walked him up the block to our house. When I returned to the park about twenty minutes later—okay, maybe it was slightly longer—I couldn't find him. In a panic, I yelled out his name. The lady who'd taken him home told me he was fine. Mamaleh didn't think so. She punished me more than I deserved, I thought. During the most gorgeous days of the year, I had to stay inside and clean up the basement. After that episode, I never again abandoned Ian or anyone else.

"So where do you live, Sylvia? I'll take you to your door."

Her gaze shifts from the foggy car windows to my face. She wrinkles her forehead in a way that shows concern about something more important than the game, if that's possible.

"Hey, is anything wrong?" I'm mortified that I might have offended her.

"No, no. All good. I'm just on the next block. Turn left here."

Sheets of rain continue to spill from the sky as we round the corner, then more lightning strikes the ground. When I can't see a metre ahead of the car, I'm forced to pull over to the curb. Wrapped in darkness, we wait for a break.

"You know," Sylvia says between claps of thunder, "the more you play with lower-level players, the more mediocre your game will be. I've noticed that when I'm on the court with weak players, I miss the easiest shots." The clattering sound of rain on the car's roof almost drowns out her quiet voice.

I hate where this conversation is going. I abhor that weaker players rarely get the respect they deserve for putting themselves out there, facing rejection, taking risks, and withstanding the pressure. But Sylvia's composure is so calming, so soft and reassuring, I don't want to break the spell by challenging her. "You may be onto something, Sylvia. Still, I think you can learn from playing with people at different levels. Besides, we were all beginners once. I remember how scary that felt."

Sylvia nods. An awkward silence falls between us. I look down at my watch, then Sylvia and I both begin to speak at once.

"Do you want…?" I begin to ask her about playing together again.

"Will you be…?" Sylvia seems to be interested in more games with me too. We laugh about thinking alike in the exact same moment.

A few minutes later, watching Sylvia make a dash for her house, I wonder if we have anything in common other than pickleball. I have no idea if she has a husband, kids, or a mother as smothering as mine. I guess it's none of my business. Yet I'm intrigued by this woman whose tranquil manner is the opposite of mine. Though I suspect that we're quite dissimilar, I drive away feeling connected to her and wonder what it would have been like to have had a sister who knew what you were thinking before the words spilled from your mouth.

Arlene R. has created a new Doubles session "PICKLES & GRUB NITE!" Social R.R. at Ramsden Park HOCKEY RINK on Friday, July 25 from 5:30PM to 8:30PM.

Arlene included the following note: PICKLES & GRUB NIGHT @ RAMSDEN. FUN TIMES! JOIN US.

After games, we walk a few blocks to a local café on Yonge Street.

I'm in, but I'm not sure for what. A pickup game or a pickup? Now that I'm a widow, there's not much to lose. And Mamaleh would be thrilled if I found a new partner. It's about time, she'd say. But she doesn't realize how old I look. It's not just the dark circles under my eyes and the drooping shoulders. I suspect that people don't see me at all. I feel like an invisible spectator watching a parade go by, except when I play pickleball.

I head down to Ramsden Park on a promising summer evening that's warm but not suffocatingly hot. Although I'm eager to play, I'm also looking forward to the social mingling. Who knew that pickleball might intersect with romance? Before I leave my condo, I slather my lips with shimmery fuchsia lipstick and put on my heart-shaped locket necklace to create the right vibe.

"Hey, what are you doing here, Heidi?" Ron calls out as soon as he sees me registering at the whiteboard tent. "I didn't know you play here."

"Just checking it out." I'm struggling to appear calmer than I feel.

"You look nice this evening," he says, moving close enough to extend his arm around my shoulder, but I step away from him, too anxious to converse.

In my first game of mixed doubles, I'm playing against a man and woman who must be twenty-five years younger than I am. Just kids. They look at me and then at each other with a mischievous exchange of smiles. My eyes twitch as I return the first serve to the opponent's corner.

"Good drive," my partner, Bill, says. I've never played with him before. He looks to be in his mid-fifties and a bit tipsy, with a squint. When my opponent's third shot veers too close to the kitchen line on my side of the net for me to retrieve, Bill races across the court to make a brilliant save.

"Wow! Great return, Bill." I'm feeling more confident about our chances of winning until I forget to move up to the kitchen line and miss the next easy return. Our opponents are watching me screw up, their expressions blank and bored. Bill explodes.

"After all I've done for you," he says. "I nearly killed myself running across the court to return that ball near the kitchen, which was yours, and now you're just standing there with leaden feet. Are you trying to make us lose?"

I detest being drawn into this angry blame game, as if I'm having a lover's spat with someone I just met. I don't even know this guy's surname. If I bumped into him wearing street clothes at the mall, I doubt I would recognize him or say hello. After three minutes of play, I'm sunk.

The rest of the game goes from bad to worse to worst. I can't shake the disdain Bill feels for me. I'm conscious of his judgment whenever my serves are too long or don't clear the kitchen line. I'm giving the game away, and we both know it.

At the end of the evening, when Ron invites me to the post-play stroll down Yonge Street to the local café, I beg off, praying that I'll be in bed before 10 p.m. Something about this form of speed dating is not working for me. I prefer to stick to my own hood, my own street, and my own peeps. Okay, Mamaleh will be disappointed that I didn't meet Prince Charming tonight. But after everything she's been through, she'll survive. She always does. The question is, will I?

Early the next morning, before my feet touch the floor, Mamaleh calls, asking me to visit her. "I want to read to you from my old writing tablet or whatever you call it before I go to my grave," she says. "You know, the writing pad that you found in my closet, the one I wrote in the DP camp when I felt lonely. Oh, and bring me a few coughing drops to wet my throat. That wouldn't hurt either, my Heidi."

I shower, gulp down tea, grab my Mac laptop, and head over to her house on Maple Drive to video-record her reading. I've brought a few Halls lozenges with me just in case.

CHAPTER 2

Mamaleh

Recording 01.mp4

1946. At school the pencil felt strange in my hand. I wasn't sure how to hold it anymore. Mother used to complain that my pencil grip was improper because my thumb always crossed over my forefinger, one of those bad habits I couldn't shake. Worse things could happen. Way worse. When nobody was looking, I rested the pencil under my nose and took a sniff. I loved the smell of a newly sharpened pencil. It was the only thing around there that seemed the tiniest bit familiar.

A lady wearing a baggy dress asked from the front of the room if we were listening, as if we were restless children instead of high school students. I was sixteen, after all.

Thin faces with haunted eyes like mine looked up at her and nodded. Sitting at long tables, we slumped over math worksheets. Too easy and silly in my opinion. I knew how to subtract. Six minus five equals one. I was there alone, minus them.

As soon as the teacher turned away, I tore a piece of paper from my tablet. I wanted to write a letter to my brother back home, but he probably wouldn't get it. The mail was too unpredictable. So were bed sheets and medicine. But the one thing I could predict: A fresh orange would never be available for breakfast in that godawful displaced persons camp. Not a chance—unless you bought it off the black market.

It was bleak that day. Sleet tortured the windowpanes. A ferocious wind hurled empty biscuit tins against the building and forced people to walk sideways. Somewhere in the nearby forest I imagined a tree being uprooted, ripped from the soil that nourished it. I pulled my skimpy sweater across my chest. An uprooted tree couldn't survive there. Impossible.

The teacher asked if Roza Lau was present. I waved my hand, but I wanted to scream so loudly that the whole world heard me. Roza Lau was a big fake. An imposter. I wasn't born Roza Lau, and I didn't want to be her. So call me by my real name, I wanted to shout— Shayna Schreiber. Shayna, not Roza. Got that? Of course, I didn't dare say what I was thinking. Father would have been furious if I had been discovered and sent back.

I told her that I was here, though I felt as absent as a lost glove. Six divided by six equals one.

I was divided from them.

The longer I stared at the floral sack this teacher lady was wearing, the more irritated I got. Her boobs jiggled every time she moved. Mother would never have stepped out of the house looking like that. She always paraded around town in her long silver fox coat, looking so glamorous. She was the most stylish person in our shtetl.

When I returned from school at the displaced persons camp in a grumpy mood, Mrs. Lau told me to try to forget. She said to put the past behind me because this was my home for now. Her voice was whispery to conceal our conversation from the other families living in the barracks with us. The walls separating our single room from the neighbours were so flimsy that nosy Gilda Goldchain next door could probably have heard every word we spoke. Anyway, I had no intention of obeying Mrs. Lau. She was only my pretend mother, a caretaker for the time being. I told Mrs. Lau that I was not going to forget a single moment of what happened in the past, and she couldn't make me so she shouldn't even try.

Then I rubbed my toes against the snapshot from home tucked inside my shoe. Still there. I rushed to my bed and felt for the envelope of photos hidden between the narrow mattress and the coil bedsprings.

I smoothed my hand over the envelope until a warm feeling rose from the photos of my family. I would have given anything to peek at the one of my big brother, Mendl. Just a quick glimpse of him would have been enough. But Mrs. Lau said it wasn't healthy to visit the past.

I always hid the envelope under the mattress for safe keeping. If anyone ever found those photos, my true identity would be exposed in a split second. Mr. and Mrs. Lau didn't look anything like my real parents in the pictures. I was a complete fraud. I raced out of the room, ran down the flight of stairs to the main floor, and let the barracks door click shut behind me. I wove through rows of two-storey buildings, the fading sunlight bouncing off their slanted roofs. When I finally arrived at Central Square, I noticed several guys huddled over a bundle of papers. Their faces looked young, but their chests were sunken in the deformed shape of old men. I stood on the edge of the group, close enough to hear an endless drone of names.

I nudged my way into the circle and asked if I could see the list they were reading from. I glanced at the crumpled page smeared with fingerprints that a guy to my left gripped. After I asked twice, he passed me a hunk of sheets.

My eyes flew over the names, hundreds of them—Fleishmann, Siegel, Rosenbaum, Richman, Silverman, Berkowitz—but I couldn't find the two names I was searching for. On the second to last page, I saw our surname. My heart began to hammer like the quick beat of a drum. I knew all along that my grandparents must still be alive because they swore that we'd be together again. But the Schreibers listed were not my grandparents, Ruth and Shimon. How could that be? I dropped the sheets on the ground and covered my face with both hands. When I looked up, there was a feisty group of young guys playing *fusbol* on a field not too far away. *Oy gevalt!* Their excitement despite everything impressed and depressed me at the same time.

Later in the evening I stumbled upon a wedding in the central square. Marriages occur regularly here—sometimes five a day—because everyone wants to move on and leave behind the past. The bride wore a dress patched together from a discarded cotton mattress cover and a veil fashioned from gauze stolen from a first-aid kit. I didn't know if she was happy or sad, if she loved this man she was about to marry or if she was marrying him because it was convenient or out of pity. I only knew that I didn't belong at this gathering of strangers. I should have been attending the wedding of my brilliant neighbour Rachel or my third cousin Shmuel, the family comedian. But they were never going to have weddings. If only I could forget about my losses, like those football players seemed able to do. Forgetfulness might be a useful thing.

I returned to the barracks to finish my overdue math homework. The lamplight was so dim that the instructions on the worksheet were hard to read. My hand trembled whenever I wrote the number six. It never used to do that. Mrs. Lau announced that it was bedtime. Roza! She raised her voice when I didn't move.

I wished she would call me by my real name, though it probably didn't matter. Everyone in that place seemed to have several versions of themselves. An old self and a new self, like ghosts rotating through a revolving door. I was one of those revolving ghosts too.

CHAPTER 3

Heidi

August 2023

She stops reading there.

I'm quiet. My chest feels tight, and I'm taking short, shallow breaths. Am I making a mistake by video-recording Mamaleh reading from the tablet she somehow managed to write in while at a displaced persons camp? Listening to her story hurts more than I imagined it would. Throughout my childhood she rarely spoke of her wartime experiences, the devastating losses in her family, and the lonely years following the conflict. Why she kept the tablet buried at the back of her closet in a scuffed briefcase all these decades, I'll never know. Some families talked a lot about what happened to them during the war. Several of my pickleball buddies whose parents are Holocaust survivors know every detail of their family's history. Other families, like ours, maintained a strict silence. The memories, I suppose, are too painful to share. When I found Mamaleh's tablet one day while organizing her shoe rack, I embraced it. My chance to discover what happened to her during that terrible time had finally arrived. But she wrote in Yiddish, of course, because that was her mother tongue. I intended to have it translated, not only for my sake, but for my boys. Whether they'd read it or not was a different matter. Before their father, Bernard, died, they were closer to his side of the family, the Steins, a clan of well-connected lawyers from Montreal. The Allens, with their heavy European accents and fondness for *Yiddishkeit*, didn't have as much gravitas. I kept my maiden name to stand my ground. I was born an Allen and would always be an Allen.

When Covid struck, during those endless days of brain fog, I had one semi-bright idea. I could capture Mamaleh reading from her tablet in Yiddish on camera and have her translate the words into English, paragraph by paragraph, as she went along. If she stumbled over a few phrases here and there, I didn't care. If the reading and translation took gobs of time, all the better. I hoped the project would be a win-win for all of us. The activity had to be more stimulating for her brain than binging on Netflix with her Filipina caregiver, Irene. I also figured that my sons would benefit from hearing the words coming from their grandmother's mouth. They would listen to her tone soften as she said the names of her lost family and feel more connected to her. The video recording would be her living legacy, a parting gift, a home movie to cherish when Mamaleh stopped speaking or breathing.

At least that was the plan. But today Mamaleh's reading goes on longer than I expect. I'm running late for pickleball. My game starts in twenty minutes, and I haven't had lunch yet. Irene serves us tuna sandwiches and salad, but I don't have time to eat. I wrap a brace around my upper forearm to support my elbow, which is showing early signs of tendinitis.

"Who's going to want you with a broken arm?" Mamaleh says, watching me strap on the brace with Velcro. "I've seen broken everything. Stay here by me, my Heidi. Rest. Relax. Why are you always rushing around like a chicken with your head cut off?"

The truth is, I feel proud to wear a brace, proud to be an injured athlete at my age. The brace indicates how hard I've worked to get here. And I'm not the only one wearing some kind of contraption. Almost everyone has something—for a wrist, knee, ankle. Whatever. We're like a ragtag army that refuses to quit fighting. What a goldmine we've created for the healthcare profession. Every time one of us falls, a physiotherapist somewhere can buy a boat.

I grab my paddle from the car, and as I hurry down the street to the courts, catching a glimpse of the painted rooster out of the corner of my eye, I roll my shoulders forward and back to warm up. The massive tractors are gone, but the sidewalks are littered with leftover bits of rubble. All it takes is a piece of concrete a couple of inches high for me to catch my foot and fall. I'm always on guard. Mamaleh put so much fear in me as a child that I can't take a step without thinking the next one might be my last.

What is the flip side of fear? I don't know, because fear is like my protective skin. Fear is my best friend and my worst enemy. It's the emotion that I know intimately, the one I rely on most often, the one she passed down to me. Sometimes I'm so scared that I'd like to dress in bubble wrap. But does it ever occur to Mamaleh that all those fears can become limitations? Her constant fearmongering is wrecking my pickleball game. I'm afraid to confront obstacles, reluctant to venture outside of my comfort zone and play difficult opponents.

The sun is shining when I swing open the court gate, but my mood is anything but sunny as we start a mixed doubles game. I feel anxious and edgy before we even begin. It's me and some new guy named James I've never seen before. We're up against Ron and Sylvia. I'm trying to concentrate, though my mind is not cooperating. I've underestimated the toll Mamaleh's tablet is taking on me.

On Ron's first serve to me, I call his shot out of bounds.

"No way," Ron yells across the court. "That was easily inside the baseline. Totally playable."

"Sorry," I shout back. "It was out by several metres. It's on my side, which means I make the call."

"You're cheating," Ron roars at me.

My heart starts to race. "Fuck you," I scream.

"Just let it go, Ron," Sylvia says. "No worries. We've got this game anyway." The pitch of her voice rises, but at least she doesn't seem to be furious at me like Ron is. I'm grateful to Sylvia for that. At least one person doesn't think I'm a monster. I feel safe with her, safer than I feel with anyone else on the court.

Then minutes later, after James and I pathetically fail to put any points on the board and lose the game, I'm so frustrated that I'm not ready to stop playing. "Gimmie another game. C'mon. Just one more, and I'll leave."

"It doesn't work that way, Heidi. You're off," Ron says. "George will take your spot. He's been waiting to play, and it's his turn."

"No way I'm coming off after that crap game. You were cheating the whole time."

"Sorry, you're off. We'll rotate you back into the next game."

"No!" I refuse to move.

"You're a disrupter," Ron says. "You've turned the court into a war zone. Thank you very much. Now get the hell off and go home."

Sylvia comes around to my side of the net. "Heidi, let's talk later. We can take a walk in the park. Okay?"

I glare at her.

"Did you bring your water bottle? Sit down and have a drink," she says. She touches my shoulder in the way one sister might soothe the other. "I may be overthinking this, but it seems like the sun has gotten to you."

"No, I'm not thirsty, but I'm starving. I missed lunch." The whole morning comes back to me—first Mamaleh reading from her tablet, then her broken arm comment, as if I'm a weird, imperfect specimen doomed to be alone forever.

"No worries," says Sylvia. "I have a protein bar from Costco you can have."

"Thanks. You've saved me. I need something to eat fast." I'm so hungry that I don't care how much sugar is in it or how many calories. As soon as I take the first bite, I feel better. Later, when Sylvia and I are strolling in the park, I tell her that my game has plateaued.

"I don't think it's just about better skills and more boring drills," I say. "On the internet it says that athletes need to optimize their mental game."

"Maybe," she says. "Whatever that means."

A young man throws a frisbee for his dog, and it lands in front of us. I jump back when the dog lurches to retrieve it.

Sylvia laughs. "That dog isn't going to hurt you."

I wonder how she knows that. I guess she didn't have a mother whose first words to her daughter were "Be careful." No, I doubt that Sylvia's mother passed down fear to her in the same way my mother did, like an infectious disease.

CHAPTER 4

Mamaleh

Recording 02.mp4

1939. The night we arrived home from our house in the country, I overheard my parents whispering about a man named Adolf. I wondered if he was the same man that I occasionally heard blaring from radios perched on windowsills overlooking the town square. Sometimes in the evening, rows of chairs lined the cobblestone streets just to hear this man describe the Germanic people as a superior Aryan race. Our Yiddish was good enough to understand the bad things he was saying in German. I shuddered from head to foot whenever I listened to him. Eavesdropping on my parents talking in the living room, I struggled to make sense of the situation. The next night, when this man cursed Jews over the radio and threatened to wipe us off the entire map of Europe, I stayed in our house, turned off the radio, and shut every window. I pretended to be escaping from a plague, like the one that was spread by fleas on black rats a long time ago. I felt sick thinking about those big rats.

Only when the Germans crossed into Szczniki did I begin to understand what was really going on. I was eating creamy porridge for breakfast at the time but dropped my spoon as soon as I heard the Nazis roll into the town centre. The ground rumbled under the weight of their tanks and armoured trucks. I rushed to the living room window to see the German soldiers on motorcycles, wearing big helmets, screech to a halt. They pointed their revolvers at neighbours, who scurried inside their houses, terror-stricken. A block away, a bunch of soldiers stomped through the laneways. Their boots slapped the dry earth, creating a storm of dust.

As the weeks passed, I became more afraid of the Nazis. They stopped Jewish men in the streets and cut off half their beards, half their moustaches, and one eyebrow to make their faces look ugly, to humiliate them. German soldiers posted notices on telegraph poles announcing that every day twenty-five men had to report for work at a special assembly point. Everyone was too scared to disobey Nazi orders. They forced the Jewish Council to collect gold, silver, foreign currency, fur coats, light bulbs, and cigarettes from us. I knew this because Father sat on the council in our shtetl. He said that the council members had no choice. They had to hand over anything valuable to the Germans. They gathered food for the German soldiers too: ten chickens daily, two hundred eggs, and large quantities of butter, cheese, and milk while we had less and less to eat. Sometimes my brother Mendl and I had to skip lunch and dinner, which made me weak and angry, but I kept quiet for my parents' sake. They had no power. What could they do about our growling stomachs, anyway?

Day by day Father became more upset. Then one morning Nazi attack dogs shredded the skin on his lower arms and drove him into the icy Rodam river. At dinner that night he insisted our family leave Szczniki at once and warned us that a safe exit was still possible, but not for much longer.

Mother refused to leave. Whenever the subject of our departure came up, she would walk away. She'd go to the window and rest her head on the windowpane, searching the deserted streets. Who are you looking for, I'd ask, but she wouldn't talk. All her fashionable skirts and blouses hung in her cupboard, unworn. She rarely left the house. Father had the *seychel* to hide her silver fox coat before the Nazis stole it from us. Thank the Almighty for his shrewd good sense. But when Father begged her to pack a few small things for our escape, Mother yelled at him to leave her alone and said she was going nowhere. She'd rather die first.

I asked if she might die before tomorrow. She said no, not for a long, long time, so not to worry about it.

Not worry? How was not worrying even possible?

CHAPTER 5

Heidi

August 2023

The more Mamaleh reads from her tablet, the more I want to hide in a rubbish bin and pretend that none of what she experienced ever happened. I may be old, but whatever she lived through still lives in me. Of course I want to preserve her memories and pass them along to my sons. I am proud of who she is and what she endured. But her grief is so complicated and disturbing. It makes me feel vulnerable, the opposite of what it takes to play pickleball. To begin playing pickleball at my age is taking a gigantic leap. It means allowing yourself to be calm and relaxed, to be exposed, to trust, to compete. And to be willing to make mistakes—lots of them—and also to be willing to fail. I wasn't born with any of those traits and skills. Under my parents' roof, I didn't develop them either.

When I hear Mamaleh stumble on some of the words in English, I know she's annoyed with me. I stop recording her and sigh, feeling helpless, then close my eyes and count to ten, fifteen, twenty, as if the passage of a few more seconds will dissolve her frustration.

"My Heidi," she says. "You and me, we are alike. We have had bad things happen to us, and we survived them. We are widows. I lost your father more than two decades ago, and I didn't sink. Neither will you. What do they say nowadays? Restart yourself. Like a car that goes kaput, take it to a mechanic for a tune-up job."

I laugh. "You don't mean restart, Mamaleh. You mean reinvent, or as they say in pickleball, reset."

"Reset. Restart. Reinvent. Re-something. You know what I mean. Go win." She flicks her wrist at me to dismiss any further discussion and asks Irene for a cup of tea to wash down her pills, with two cubes of sugar but no cookies unless Irene has made her chocolate rugelach. Of course Irene makes Mamaleh her favourite pastry because nobody is a more devoted caregiver than Irene Santos.

That afternoon when our Thursday pickleball session comes to an end, I tell Sylvia about the funny conversation I had with my mother. "So she's basically telling me I need help, like a coach or someone who can give me a boost."

"A coach? You mean for life or pickleball?" Sylvia asks.

"For everything, starting with pickleball."

"A pickleball coach?" Sylvia sounds skeptical. "What for? Just look at the millions of pickleball videos on YouTube. Everything you need to know about the game is only a click away."

"Thanks for the hot tip, Sylvia, but no thanks. Circumstances and players are obviously unique."

"In my experience," she says, "and I may be wrong about this, the only way you get better is by playing and practicing. Time-on-task is the best strategy to improve your game without spending big bucks on a fancy coach."

"Time-on-task! You're kidding, right. Malcolm Gladwell says it takes ten thousand hours to achieve mastery of anything. I may be incontinent and bedridden before I get around to logging that many pickleball hours."

I'm convinced that unflappable Sylvia just doesn't get it. To break my cycle of fear and defeat—to learn to win—I'll need help. On the drive home from the courts, I stop at Shoppers Drug Mart because it's Seniors' Day, and there's a twenty percent discount on regularly priced items. I purchase a can of hairspray to coat the face of my pickleball paddle. Presumably the hairspray will increase the spin on my pickleball shots. Okay, it's not kosher and probably won't work. But what the hell. Like Mamaleh tells me, I must become the mistress of self-reinvention. I must reset. Correction. She'd never say that.

Re-something, my Heidi. Win already. That's more like her.

"Nice," I say to Sylvia when we walk through the double glass doors at Oakridge Tennis and Racquet Club, where we've agreed to meet our highly recommended pickleball coach, Jonathan Craig. Despite Sylvia's initial resistance, I'm able to convince her that a one-hour session with a professional would be a game changer for both of us.

"C'mon," I coax her. "It'll transform your life."

We agree to split the cost. And I promise her lunch at Café Landwer afterward.

"My third son, Simon, used to play here when he was a kid," I tell Sylvia, remembering the long waits for him and the astronomical cost of his tennis lessons. "The two of us sometimes knocked around a tennis ball together back then."

Sylvia seems disinterested. Too much information, I suppose.

"How about you? Any kids?"

She indicates no with a small shake of her head and a forced smile.

I'm afraid to burden Sylvia with any further minutia about Simon, though I'd like to tell her that he refuses to play pickleball with me now that I'm old. I imagine he's thinking an old woman is not supposed to be chasing balls across a court. She should realize that her bones are brittle and she could fall and break a hip or a wrist. An old woman is not supposed to behave like a young woman, exposing her legs in short, pleated sports skirts with half of her bum sticking out. She should realize that her body is of no interest to anyone, and it should be kept covered. I can almost hear Simon thinking, Act your age, Mom.

As if he regards aging and its effects as some sort of personal failing.

"So," Sylvia says, interrupting the chatter in my head. "Your son Simon is a racquet guy. Maybe he'll play pickleball with you."

"Never. He's far too advanced in racquet sports for me. Besides, pickleball is below his athletic pay grade. The game doesn't have the panache of tennis."

"Not yet," she says. "But you never know."

"Wrong, Sylvia. There will never be the pickleball equivalent to Wimbledon with the British royal family watching from their exclusive Royal Box. If Queen Elizabeth were alive, would she ever turn up in Brixton to see some fanatic picklers play mixed doubles? No fucking way."

Once inside Oakridge we meet Jonathan Craig, who is waiting for us at the check-in counter. He is a tall, muscular, sixty-something dude who looks like he's spent too much of his life pumping iron in a gym and hitting balls on a tennis court. His eyes are deep-set, and his salt-and-pepper hair is impeccably coiffed. I notice that the fourth finger of his left hand is unencumbered. No wedding band in sight.

For the lesson he pairs us with two women Sylvia and I don't know. We exchange a dubious look when we're introduced to them. One is wearing a shitload of eye makeup and two strands of pearls. When she misses a simple dink, she belly laughs and assures Jonathan that she's not always a clumsy ox. I am not amused.

Jonathan's attention, however, rarely strays from Sylvia, whose demeanour is serenely understated. She takes our opponents' gaffes in stride, the expression on her face remaining neutral. Her clothing today, as always, consists of a simple, shapeless white top and slouchy denim shorts with a leather belt. Several times Jonathan compliments Sylvia on her serves and lobs. By the end of the session, he is calling her Syl. As we walk off the court, I hear him asking if she'd be interested in additional coaching. He suggests an outdoor lesson one evening in the park.

"Sounds nice," she says in a tone so seductively sweet that she might as well be offering Jonathan double-chocolate ice cream with fudge swirled throughout. I feel jealous and excluded. The coaching session did nothing to diminish my court fears or improve my game. In fact I feel more deflated while Sylvia, who had to be cajoled and bribed into attending, is now basking in confidence.

"Have you lost your ability to think?" I say to her over a late lunch. "I hope you're bringing pepper spray with you if you're having an evening pickleball lesson with Jonathan. What if he's a sexual predator? Women never think enough about their personal safety."

"Don't be absurd." She rolls her eyes at me, like I'm the irrational one. "He's a former tennis player turned pickleball coach, not a rapist or a mass murderer. And if you're worried about women's safety and security, you might want to ponder the risks of online dating."

"Don't try to change the subject, Sylvia. This coach Jonathan, who was a total stranger an hour ago, just asked you on a date. My late husband, Bernard, may he rest in peace, would have been up in arms, though he never had trouble leaving me alone while he played golf all weekend."

"I'm going to have a pickleball lesson with Jonathan, Heidi, not a date," Sylvia says between bites of avocado toast. "And at least I know that Jonathan is a real person with a job and a certifiable identity, which is better than the false identities men assume on those online dating apps, like Hinge. You know what catfishing is, right?"

"Why are you avoiding the real issue here by talking about all this online dating stuff. You're married, right?" My appetite for the Mediterranean salad I ordered is dwindling fast.

"Very married, you could say, and I don't see a pickleball coach interfering with my marriage one iota. Nor is a discussion of online dating a betrayal of my husband. It's out there. That's all I'm saying, and women can get hurt by it. Now can we stop talking about dating and relationships? Let's find a lighter topic."

"Okay. Have you read any good books lately? I don't even know if you like to read."

Sylvia puts down the remaining half of her avocado toast and begins tugging on her wedding ring, as if she's trying to remove it from her finger. I'm not sure why. "Yes, I'm a big reader," she says. "I mainly read novels. Long ones that I can escape into, like the Russian classics. Tolstoy is my favourite. And you?"

"Interesting. I also read, but more nonfiction, especially history. European history is my thing. I'll devour anything on the French

Revolution. Liberty, equality…that's what speaks to me, if you know what I mean."

Sylvia doesn't comment. She continues to fiddle with her wedding ring. When the band won't slide over her knuckle, she brings the ring to her lips and holds it there for several seconds while I pay the tab for lunch.

CHAPTER 6

Sylvia

August 2023

I can barely open my eyes this morning. Seven and a half hours in bed, and I'm still tired. Tired of hearing Danny walk and talk in his sleep, tired of turning the toaster upside down to shake my husband's stale bread crumbs from that grungy appliance, tired of wiping his piss off the toilet bowl rim, tired of the drudgery of housework with no help. I need to get away from here. Shut the door and swap the whole thing—home, husband, garden—for pickleball. To my list of thirty ways to abandon my husband, I'm adding this note to self: Just go for the dill, Syl. I won't explain much of the game to him. Why bother? He's not really listening.

As I walk toward the door, Danny calls after me. "Where are you going?"

"To a pickle lesson." I glance back at him working his way through a bag of peanuts in the living room. He drops peanut skins on the carpet as he eats.

"Who's the instructor?"

"Jonathan Craig." I glance at my phone to check for a text message from him. He's probably wondering if I'm still coming or just running late.

"Who's he? Do I know this Jonathan who you can't seem to live without? You're in love with him, right."

"I told you about Jonathan already. He's the coach I had for a pickleball lesson at Oakridge, and no, I am not in love with him." I twirl my keychain around my finger, waiting for the predictable next question.

"I must have forgotten his name." Danny gives me a sheepish look, then pivots to less embarrassing ground. "Anyway, there's a coach for everything these days. Careers, happiness, even strengthening your bones. So what's for dinner?"

I sigh. "Chili. It's on the stove. Salad is in the fridge."

"Only you and this Jonathan?"

"No, I asked my friend Heidi to come along. You know, the woman who drove me home in the rain one day."

"I don't remember her either. Who's she?" Danny looks uncomfortable again, which makes me feel guilty that I've somehow diminished him. How ridiculous! Belittling Danny is the last thing I intend to do. He, on the other hand, never misses an opportunity to disparage me.

"Don't worry about it," I say. "See you later."

"When will you be back?"

"In an hour or two."

"Make it one, Sylvia. And I mean on the dot."

I drag my feet along the pavement, irritated by Danny's heavy-handed control, until I round the corner on Maple Drive and my spirit lifts. In the park the baseball parents cheer on their kids. All the courts are in use. I spot Jonathan and Heidi in a fierce rally. Jonathan turns his head to greet me, but Heidi, focused on the rhythmic back and forth of the ball, is too absorbed to say hello.

"Very good, Heidi," I say to encourage her. "You'll be a pro in no time."

Jonathan winks and waves me onto the court for drills. He looks buff in his sleeveless muscle shirt, which exposes a heart tattoo on his left bicep. It's not a traditional heart shape, like the neon hearts that people hung in their windows during Covid. No, no. Jonathan has a complex heart etched on his arm with valves, chambers, and ventricles. In one of our previous engagements (sans Heidi), he told me the anatomical heart is a symbol of life, love, and the preciousness of each heartbeat. Okay. To me that suggests Heidi is wrong about Jonathan. My gut tells me there's nothing to fear with this guy. He's not a violent or cruel type. In the department of intimate partner abuse, I trust my instincts.

On the court Jonathan lectures us as he returns our dinks at the kitchen line. "Pickleball, like any other sport, takes technical skill and tactical awareness. It's a game of finesse, not just powerful smashes."

"That's very interesting, Jonathan, and I truly don't mean to be rude"—I take a big breath—"but can we speed things up a bit and play a game? I'm sorry, but I don't have much time tonight."

"Not so fast, Syl," Jonathan says. I hear a tiny flare of disappointment in his voice. "You don't want to get too fixated on performance at your level. Think about yourself as an acorn with the potential to be a magnificent oak tree."

I don't remember putting acorns and potential on the agenda for tonight's lesson. In fact, I have an abiding disinterest in self-improvement and don't appreciate someone pushing it on me. If anyone here is smitten with the idea of potential, it's Heidi, not me. She's hanging on Jonathan's every word as if he's delivering Christ's Sermon on the Mount. Oh my God. She can't stop bobbing her head in agreement, like a robot on drugs.

The minutes are vanishing, and I feel more and more frustrated with Jonathan's preaching until he finally switches the topic of the lesson from the ethereal to something more grounded—footwork, which he tells us, is the most underdeveloped technique in the game. He demonstrates the split step for quick movements in any direction, the shuffle for lateral movement across the court, and the cross-step for reaching wide backhand shots. Very impressive, I think. Jonathan really knows his stuff and, despite the self-improvement spiel, his heart is in the right place. Yet I find it hard to keep my head in the game when I know my domineering husband is counting down the clock. *Get home on time or else…*

On the next court, four guys shriek, curse, and grunt as they blast the pickleball at each other. Also, a couple of unruly young men, waiting for their turn to play, hover around the edges of our court, guzzling beer and tossing the empty cans over the fence into the bushes.

"When are you going to be done?" A guy yells at us from the bench.

"We just started playing," Heidi says. She's practicing her split step in her returns to Jonathan, unwilling to forego a minute of play. "We signed up on the Pickleball Organizer for one hour. Until then, you can kindly bug off."

"So fucking what if you signed up on the Pickleball Organizer," the guy shouts back. "It's not a court reservation system, Ms. Know-It-All."

"Then what the hell is it?"

"It's an organizing app to help people create and join games with other players—duh! These are public courts with a half-hour time limit. Read the sign on the fence, lady. You've got thirty minutes, starting now. I just put my paddle on the peg to reserve the next court."

To intimidate us, he takes out his phone and begins to shoot a video of Jonathan, Heidi, and me. Someone else walks his bike onto the side of our court, stands there with his arms folded, and follows each of our shots with an exaggerated turn of his head.

Jonathan, who seems to sense a confrontation, asks Heidi and me if we want to reschedule for an afternoon next week. I decline. I have a feeling that tonight the park is a safer option than going home. Watching Jonathan and Heidi prepare to leave, I hesitate, then make a snap decision.

"Hey, guys," I call out to the next court. "Does anyone happen to have an extra beer?"

Before I walk over to get it, Heidi explodes. "What in the hell are you doing, Sylvia? You can't hang out with them." Her bossiness reminds me of my annoying older sister, who tends to treat me like a thumb-sucking baby in need of protection.

"You and Jonathan can go when you're done," I tell her. "I'm taking a little break before I head home."

"It's pitch black in the park. Those guys are drunk and a century younger than you are."

Heidi's voice is becoming shrill. "Let me drive you home," she begs.

Jonathan says, "Or I can give you a lift, Syl. I really want to make sure you're safe."

Heidi presses on. "You said you didn't have much time tonight. C'mon. We'll leave now and be at your house in a minute."

"I'm fine," I assure them. "In fact, I'll have more fun here than I would at home. Just leave. I'll get home by myself when I'm ready."

"I insist, Sylvia." Heidi again. "We're leaving this park together."

"No offence, Heidi, but don't you think I'm old enough to make decisions for myself?"

"Sylvia! You're possessed."

"I'm fine. Please get off your high horse and let me be."

"You are not fine. What's going on with you?"

"We can't abandon you here," Jonathan says. "I can't."

"I've got this paddle for armour." I hold up my pickleball paddle to hide the tears burning under my eyelashes.

"A lot of good that flimsy thing will do you." Heidi shakes her head. "Be reasonable, Sylvia. Please."

"There are many ways to use a pickleball paddle," I say. "It can be a fan, a fly swatter, a back scratcher, a shield, and, if necessary, a lethal weapon. Now please, please leave me alone and go."

Jonathan walks toward me. "I'm not leaving without you. I honestly can't." He reaches for my arm to pull me close to him.

"Go!" I put up my hand to stop him and offer a brave smile. "Leave. I absolutely insist. I'll text you later."

Which I do not do, because when I return home later, my husband is sitting on the living room sofa waiting for me.

"You smell like a brewery," he says, glaring at me. Then he gets up and walks across the room. Without warning, he slaps my face twice and grabs the pickleball bag from my shoulder. "Did you have fun playing with your friend Jonathan? You will never play that bullshit game again."

In the bathroom I put a cold washcloth on my face to reduce the swelling. I know that I'm going to feel awful all night. It's going to come in ripples of nausea—stronger, then weaker, then stronger again, the sour churning in my stomach, the anguished feeling of shame and regret, the throbbing in my head, the bruises on my cheeks. I squeeze my eyes shut as if I can make the ugliness disappear.

What will I tell Heidi and Jonathan if they come to our house to check on me? And how will I tell them I'm finished with pickleball?

I can't say that because I'm not going to quit. More and more, I'm convinced that the best way to break loose of this nightmare is to stay in the game.

CHAPTER 7

Heidi

August 2023

Debbie G. has organized a new Doubles session at Maple Drive Park for Thursday, August 17 from 4:00 PM to 6:00 PM. Click here to get specific details and join us.

When I sign up, I'm relieved to see that Sylvia's name is listed on the schedule, but with a strange note:

Does anyone have a paddle I can borrow? I lost mine and haven't had time to get to Sporting Life to buy a new one. Grateful for the short-term loan. Sylvia

Okay, she lost her paddle. I can live with that. She's lucky she didn't lose her life with those drunk thugs in the park. What was gentle Sylvia doing with them, anyway? She's old enough to be their grandmother. Why would any twenty-something want to hang out with her, and why in the name of God would she want to go anywhere near them?

Still, it's hard to believe she lost her paddle. She always seems to be in control of her possessions. She's not the type to search desperately for her protective goggles in her tote bag. They're always in the bag's outer pocket. She doesn't leave her sweatshirt on the bench, like I do. She always ties it around her shoulders when she leaves the court. No, Sylvia is careful not to lose things. Loss doesn't haunt her. It doesn't define her. That's my hang up, which, as the expression goes, I come by honestly.

I only wish Sylvia would be more vigilant at night in the park. You never know what stranger might be lurking in the bushes or walking behind you on Maple Drive. Careful. That's what Mamaleh reminds me every time I leave her house. Careful. This time she's right.

I can barely see Sylvia's face when she shows up for the game on the seventeenth. She's wearing a baseball cap pulled down as far as possible on her forehead and cat-eye sunglasses with oversized lenses and upswept corners. At first, I think she's wisely shielding her skin from the late afternoon sun. But as I move closer to lend her my extra paddle, I see that she's applied too much heavy concealer to her face. The goop has cracked along the folds on either side of her nose, exposing bluish purple bruising close to the surface.

Extending my second paddle to her, I feel obligated to ask, "So where did those bruises on your face come from?"

"From the dermatologist who sprayed my sun spots the other day with liquid nitrogen." She tugs on her baseball cap, perhaps to conceal more of the facial discoloration.

I look at her, expecting an explanation. She can't think I believe that unconvincing answer. Yes, liquid nitrogen may cause redness, a bit of swelling and blistering, but not the amount of bruising I can see around Sylvia's cheekbones. The muscle in her jaw flexes as she clenches her teeth. She seems to be searching for words that won't come.

"Is there something you want to tell me, Sylvia? Something I can do?" Her gaze holds mine, and for a second, I'm mortified that I've made a mistake by prying into her personal life and betraying her trust. I know she hates being bossed around or told what to do, especially by a sisterly, know-it-all type like me. So last week when

Sylvia accompanied me to my auto mechanic's garage for a brake check and oil change, she decided to give me a taste of my own medicine. We were watching a soccer game on the television he always has on, and I commented on the lean physique of one of the players. Sylvia seized the moment. If you're so keen on the male form, she'd snapped, why don't you do something proactive about your own needs and back off my case.

Now, staring at Sylvia's swollen face, I'm speechless. "I'll be fine, Heidi," she says. "Trust me."

The late afternoon sun radiates such fierce heat that I feel wonky. Perhaps my perception of Sylvia is distorted, or the woman facing me isn't Sylvia at all. She's someone else I've never met before. A hint of clarity would be helpful, but I'm afraid that my continual probing will make matters worse. Forget that. What if Sylvia's in trouble?

Without further dithering and no soft pedalling, I blurt out: "Is someone physically abusing you?"

That pulsing in her jaw starts up again, as if she's trying to supress what she's feeling. Her grip on the paddle tightens. Throwing back her shoulders, she says, "Let's play."

I sigh. "Look, Sylvia. If you're being abused, you need to call the police. I know this is a terrible thing for us to discuss, but I'm really worried about what's happening to you."

She gestures for me to move backward, indicating that she isn't interested in my sympathy or support. "Do you want to play the first game with me or not?"

"I always want to play with you," I say. We're up against two players who are light-years ahead of us in hand speed and reflexes. Even Jonathan's coaching around the clock would do nothing to close the gap between us and them. A thin layer of sand on the court's surface increases my fear of falling. Even if I wanted to, I can't implement the footwork patterns Jonathan tried to teach us. To nobody's surprise, we lose.

Walking off the court after our defeat, I offer Sylvia a drink of water, but she says no. I feel wretched. Not only did we play a terrible game, but I made Sylvia feel worse by asking about her face. She missed easy shots to her forehand and didn't return one backhand the entire game. I'm sorry that I raised the issue of physical abuse with her instead of keeping my mouth shut.

I take another swig of water and follow Sylvia's gaze toward the path. She's watching a guy heading in our direction. As he comes closer, she packs up her court shoes, takes a sweatshirt out of her bag, and slips it on. Is this young man a son she's never mentioned? He's hobbling along with an assistive cane. A knapsack sits high on his back.

"Who's that?" I ask. "The way he's looking at you scares the shit out of me. Do you know him?"

"I met him in the park the other night. Don't you remember seeing him? His name is Joe. Nice guy. Really, everything's okay, so calm down." She speaks to me in a tone that might be used to reassure an anxious dog.

"No, I don't recall seeing anyone with a cane that night. Joe who?"

Sylvia doesn't bother to introduce me to Joe, which I take as an ominous sign. Before I have a chance to ask where she's going, they leave the court together and turn left instead of our usual right at the park's exit. I text her several times, but my messages are unread. Also, she forgot to return the paddle I loaned her. You're welcome, I want to screech at her.

By the time I arrive at Mamaleh's house for a visit, my head is spinning, and I've forgotten to pick up her prescription at the pharmacy. I check my text messages every three minutes, but there's no response from Sylvia. Nada.

CHAPTER 8

Mamaleh

Recording 03.mp4

1942. *Baruch HaShem*. Thank God. Father and Mother survived the mass murder. They were almost the only people in our town who did. They had gone to synagogue to celebrate Rosh Hashanah with the other Jews, but they escaped by jumping out a window and running away. Father quickly dispatched a shepherd boy to collect my brother and me from the safe house where we were hiding. On a riverbank outside of town, we joined them. Bodies lay not far from where we sat. When I asked Father why these people were sleeping by the river, he said that they were resting peacefully, and I shouldn't disturb them. Were they getting up soon, I wondered. Mother wrapped her arms around me from behind and put her hands over my eyes so I wouldn't stare at the lifeless bodies. They weren't sleeping. I felt a sob creep into my throat, but I didn't want that sob to escape in front of them.

Mother and Father each took one of my hands and lifted me to my feet. My body felt like limp lettuce. Mendl took off his suit jacket, rumpled from sleeping in it, and put it around my shoulders. With night coming soon, we began to walk toward the next village, where we hoped to find food and a place to sleep. Father carried me most of the way.

When we arrived, we slipped under the barbed-wire fence of the ghetto created by the Nazis in the oldest and dirtiest part of the town.

Garbage, loose bricks, and glass from broken windows littered the empty streets. I asked where everybody was. Father said there were curfews. The Nazis ordered Jews to stay inside as soon as the sun went down. Anyone who tried to escape from the ghetto would be harshly punished.

He pulled us into the first barn he saw. Many other families already lived there. Each grouping claimed a small patch of space. They strung up old potato sacks to separate themselves from their neighbours, so we could hear them speaking Yiddish but not see them. In the morning, everyone began moving about. I wanted to know why they were all wearing a yellow star. Rolling over in the hay, my brother said it was so the Nazis could identify who was a Jew, obviously. He didn't explain why. Then Mother arrived with a cup of water mixed with some weeds for breakfast. She said we would be leaving soon because the Nazis were going to destroy the ghetto any day now. I asked how they would destroy this whole place. She said they would clear out the barns and apartments where Jews were living and send everyone with a yellow star to a far worse area than this.

I was scared because Mother looked like a skeleton. The stylish outfit she had worn to synagogue was filthy and loose on her. She cried a lot so I didn't want to bother her, but I needed to know where we were going. She told me that we were going to hide in a pit below the ground on the estate of a Polish landowner.

That night, when the guard in the ghetto dropped off to sleep, Father waved for us to follow him along a path to a clump of trees concealing part of the ghetto fence. We slithered on our stomachs under the barbed wire, like a...like a *shlang* moving in the grass. A snake! Dirt from the ground made a crust on my lips. When I swallowed, a glob of mud stuck at the back of my throat. Then Father told us to run. The Nazis were not far behind. We could hear their boots thudding through the forest. As I stood up, my leg caught on a branch in the dense underbrush. Blood spurted from the gash. I slowed down to wipe it with the sleeve of my best dress. I was too afraid to stop running. Father helped me limp the rest of the way to the pit on the Polish estate. All the while, warm red liquid oozed down my leg.

CHAPTER 9

Heidi

August 2023

That gash on Mamaleh's leg never seemed to heal completely. While she reads from her tablet, I lean toward her, trying to find the scar it left on her calf. My hand slides up and down until I find the little bump. As a kid, I liked touching it because the rest of the skin on her leg felt like the bristles on a brush rather than soft and smooth. I used to ask her about the bump. I wanted to know how she got it, and if it hurt. She'd always assured me that it was just a little scar. I didn't need to worry about it, she'd say. But sometimes when I touched it, I did worry. What if her small bump suddenly jumped to my leg and became my scar? What if it spread across my entire body? I'd be scarred for life.

Irene doesn't move during the reading. Only her eyebrows lift as the details of Mamaleh's childhood spill off the page. Irene dabs at her eyes. She is a nurse by training, overqualified for the homecare she provides for Mamaleh, and underpaid too. Yet Irene stays in the job. She struggles to send monthly payments back to the Philippines to support her son and her parents, but she refuses to work in a long-term care facility where she might be paid more because she would also be more likely to get Covid. She once told me that her worst nightmare is being sent home in a casket. Her family depends on her. She is their lifeline.

As soon as Mamaleh stops reading, she reaches for Irene's hand. "A *glazele tay*, if you would be so kindly." Irene understands that my mother wants tea.

Irene hurries to the kitchen and returns with the steamy drink in a glass cup and a cube of sugar in a quaint silver bowl. She puts the sugar cube between Mamaleh's teeth and lifts the tea to her lips.

"Such a sad story," Irene says while Mamaleh takes small sips. "Your family suffered too much. Your poor mommy running through the forest. What was her name?"

"Miriam. Heidi looks just like her," Mamaleh says. "Especially her green-brown eyes, whatever you call that colour. And Heidi is stubborn like her too."

Irene beams one of her angelic looks at Mamaleh, as if she's in the presence of a war hero. And it's true. Mamaleh and every survivor of the Holocaust acted heroically many times over. But picturing Mamaleh and her mother—Miriam, the fashionista grandmother I never knew—slithering on their stomachs in mud to escape from the Nazis is so freighted with danger that I can't shake the fear it triggers in my brain. I feel a sickening rush of adrenalin. A drop of sweat trickles at the base of my spine, like I'm there with my mother and grandmother having a near death experience too.

I'm grateful that they didn't die in the muck when they escaped from the ghetto. They lived to see the light of another day, but ultimately I lost my grandmother Miriam and my grandfather Haim. My father's parents were killed during the war too, though he rarely spoke of them. What a hole those losses left in our family. When other kids at school went to their bubbie and zaydie's house for Chanukah, we stayed home. My friend Lily celebrated Shabbat every Friday night at her grandparents' house. We stayed home. Jenny and Robin always had big Thanksgiving meals with their grandparents, but my family sat alone on Maple Drive. Once, when Mamaleh asked me to set the table for Passover, I opened the glass doors of the china cabinet and lifted out the plates we used only for that holiday. But rather than setting four dinner plates and four soup bowls around the oval table, I filled the entire table with as many plates and soup bowls as I could find to represent all the missing family who would never be able to join our seder. Such a pathetic substitute all those dishes were for our lost relatives. Mamaleh was aghast at what I did. She insisted that I return all the extra place settings to the cabinet. "Nothing will bring them back," she said. "So stop trying."

The more intensely Mamaleh engages with her past, the more I realize this recording project I suggested was a mistake. Revisiting her stories of growing up during the war elicits so much sadness in Mamaleh, and in Irene too. They both know the pain of family disruption, although their experiences and circumstances are different. Still, it's a bond they share. Listening to these dark tales also provokes a mix of anxiety and fear in me. Can what happened to Mamaleh occur again? Sometimes memories should be left alone, I suppose. Better to leave the past in the past. But it's too late to turn off the spigot of Mamaleh's memory now that the waters have begun to flow. With any luck, pickleball will serve as an antidote to the pain that her stories unleash. Bloody hell. I'm going to be late for my game.

CHAPTER 10

Sylvia

August 2023

Joe and I slow our steps along Maple Drive to accommodate his wobbly gait. I'm tempted to ask him if he recently injured his leg. But I gather from his stern facial expression that he's not in the mood for talking. At the bus stop on Bathurst, he looks at me, locking his eyes on mine, then passes me his knapsack. My stomach feels like a small, hard ball. Maybe this whole escapade is simply an enormous self-deception on my part, yet another attempt to prove that I'm not worthless. No, it's real. I hate myself more than I ever have. Right before I climb the steps of the southbound bus, Joe gives me his cane. He whispers, "Use it well."

There's not a seat available. Leaning forward and craning my neck, I notice Joe through the window. He's picking up speed—no sign of a limp—eyes cast downward as he lengthens his strides. He can't possibly see me wave goodbye to him. On the bus I'm surrounded by tired faces. We scarcely have space to breathe, like we are crushed sardines in a can. Maybe that's why I feel so vulnerable on the number 7 today. It's odd because I've been riding this bus by myself from the time I was fourteen years old with no worries whatsoever. Back then I used to go shopping at Lawrence Plaza on

Saturdays alone, always alone. No bestie then, or now for that matter, except for Heidi. (I hope she's still my friend.) Hanging out with a pal at the mall would have been much more fun than wandering around by myself, but I was too shy and insecure to make it happen. "Sylvia," my mother used to nag, "why don't you pick up the phone and ask someone to go shopping with you? Why can't you be popular like your sister? She has a million friends, and you don't have one." That hurt. I'd lie and tell her I was meeting Susan and Jennifer at the plaza that very afternoon. Over the years, twisting the truth became habit forming. I developed into a good liar. I could convince people of almost anything. At work, I occasionally talked my way out of overtime by claiming a family emergency, and my boss always believed me.

And now here I am, riding the southbound Bathurst bus once again, but caught in a much bigger lie. But what choice do I have? Danny confiscated the keys to the car. Next he'll find a way to deny me access to our bank account and take away the house keys so I'm broke and homeless.

Then what?

The bus jolts to a sudden halt at Wilson. Passengers utter half-hearted apologies as they stumble and bump into one another other and accidentally step on each other's toes. I glance up and find myself within a metre of a man I vaguely recognize from the courts on Maple Drive, Joe's curly-haired friend whom everyone calls Curls for short. His dark eyes stare right through me. I feel so shaken that I drop Joe's cane. When I retrieve it from the floor, I look up at him again, quizzically this time, and scan the bus for other recognizable faces. I wonder if I should try to elbow my way off the bus at Wilson, but I hesitate when he smiles at me, his head cocked a little to one side. I don't know how to react to his smile, because I don't know what it means or what he wants from me.

When the bus terminates at Bathurst Station, I feel the phone Joe slipped into my sweatshirt pocket buzzing. I tuck the cane under my arm and take out the new phone. I start reading a cascade of texts from Joe.

> Hey, Sylvia. Follow Curls. No talk. Walk 3 steps behind. Position cane to yr side and bit forward. Plant cane firmly on ground before stepping forward with yr dominant leg. You got this

> My eyes on u, Sylvia. U don't see me but I see u. Yr doing great. Trust me.

> Don't look around, Sylvia. Stay close behind Curls. Go where he goes

> $$$$$ soon! U'll be happy you helped me out

I'm shaking so much that the phone jitters in my hand. The hairs are standing up on the back of my neck. I can't remember ever feeling this scared in my entire life. I push the phone back into my sweatshirt pocket and rub my eye with my free palm, trying to concentrate. Is what I'm doing horrible, pointless, and reckless? Heidi would likely say yes to all three. She, Jonathan, and the pickleball players seem a million miles away from here. I've entered a world so different from them that they would never believe it.

I do exactly what Joe tells me to do. I trail closely behind Curls as he enters the Second Cup on Bloor near Bathurst. My legs are trembling. I'm shaking all over. It must be an adrenalin rush. My heart just won't slow down. I follow Curls into the coffee shop and stand next to him when he orders an Americano to go. He reaches into his pocket for some coins to pay for it, then drops a loonie on the ground. As he bends over to pick up the money, he leaves a small package at his feet. The phone Joe gave me buzzes again.

> Pick up pkg and read address. Put pkg in knapsack, zip it up. Walk slowly to address. Use cane

> Ring bell. Give knapsack to man at door. Name Charles. He is waiting for u

> Return home on bus. Meet me at bus stop

I follow every order that Joe gives me. I'm good at that. I look so respectable that nobody would suspect me of anything. Obviously, women have more freedom than men in this line of work, especially if you're as old as I am. No police officer is going to consider a senior limping along Bloor with a cane in the midafternoon as a possible drug courier. The police are more likely to think I should be at home taking a nap. Even if I had drugs in the bulging pocket of my sweatshirt, I doubt the police would look twice at me. I'm too old. I just don't fit the profile of a drug trafficker. Membership in the club of oldsters has its privileges. As long as Joe keeps me out of the spotlight and doesn't ask me to ingest illicit substances for the purpose of smuggling, I'm fine with this job. I can be the perfect pawn.

Less than ten minutes later, I tap the specified doorbell on Albany Avenue. The short, sharp, urgent ring startles me. I blink and jerk my head back.

"You must be Sylvia," the guy who opens the door says. "I'm Charles. I was expecting you." He has a deranged look to him. He's pale with hair that's long and unkempt. I hesitate at the doorway, unsure of whether to respond or just hand over the knapsack to him without any polite chit-chat. The truth is, I can't speak, can't move. I'm numb with fear. I hear teenage girls walking along the street, laughing. A loud car radio sends a song out the window. I envy the sounds of normal life. The distant wail of a police siren on Bloor propels me to act. I drop the knapsack at the guy's feet and race down the creaking stairs of his semi. I rush down Albany to Bloor without using the cane or making eye contact with anyone. On Bloor I sidle up to one of the shops and drop the cane Joe thrust into my hand less than an hour ago, pushing it with my foot as close to the building as I can. I'm ashamed that I impersonated a senior with a mobility impairment to complete a drug deal.

Hello, contemptible me.

Riding north on the Bathurst bus, I berate myself for becoming involved with this seedy character Joe and his disgusting drug deals. What have I gotten myself into? Once I was a decent woman with a good job at an accounting firm and a good name. Now I'm Joe's drug accomplice. Just like that. How totally, utterly unbelievable. I'm so confused. I'm not even sure why I'm doing this. What purpose does it serve?

Joe is waiting for me at the bus stop near Maple Drive. He nods approvingly when I descend the stairs of the bus and stand in front of him. "All good. Where's the cane?"

"I dumped it on Bloor. It's not right to impersonate a disabled person for illegal purposes, you know." He seems surprised by my sudden moral righteousness, but for once I don't care. "Next time, no cane. I have standards. Pretending to be impaired is something I refuse to do."

"Follow me," he says. At the back of an apartment building, he hands me an envelope, which I'm too scared to open at first. Then turning away from him, I pull out the unglued flap and remove the bills. As I count the meagre amount of money, I feel crestfallen. I've sold my soul for a mere pittance that won't even cover the cost of a one-way train ticket from Toronto to Windsor.

I hurry across Bathurst Street and up Maple Drive toward home. For a split second when I pass the pickleball courts, I become one of those exuberant players once again, revelling in the thwack of the ball on a well-placed serve. Where are Heidi and Jonathan now, I wonder. Even in my shameful state, I long to be playing with them.

CHAPTER 11

Mamaleh

Recording 04.mp4

1942. I'll never forget the place we stayed on a Polish estate. It was nothing more than a hovel burrowed into the earth under a pigsty. Nobody in our family could stand upright in it. It was so small that my brother, Mendl, couldn't stretch out his legs to sleep. Straw lined the damp mud floor where we slept and ate. Instead of a toilet we used a pail in the corner, which had to be emptied every evening. The smell of piss and poop never went away.

During safe hours we climbed out of the pit to work on the estate—churning butter, making ropes, and repairing boots. As soon as the estate owner gave a warning, we disappeared, like mice crawling into the woodwork. We scampered through a makeshift tunnel, sometimes remaining underground for days, trapped in the foul air. My brother feared we would all die of suffocation. Who would bury our bodies if that happened? Did anyone have a burial plan or any plan whatsoever?

Meanwhile, the wound on my leg looked like a big swollen hole, oozing yellowy pus. Itchy red skin surrounded it. Father and Mother said not to worry because a scab would eventually form and the whole mess would someday disappear.

We lost track of time underground. Had five, nine, or eleven months passed since we arrived? Maybe more. The days blurred together. Two weeks ago felt like two years ago. And what difference did it make if it was Tuesday or Thursday, April or June, nine thirty in the morning or five o'clock in the afternoon? Nobody cared. Time meant nothing to us.

When winter arrived, the air in the pit became so cold that we could see our own breath. If we ventured above ground on a snowy day, we tiptoed to avoid leaving a visible sign, I mean a print of our shoes in the snow. One morning my brother noticed a boy with a broom trailing not far behind us. He swept the thick, fresh snowflakes over our tracks until all evidence of our existence vanished. I asked who he was, and my brother told me he was the son of the estate owner.

The next time we went above ground, I hung back when my family headed for the barn to do their chores. I saw the Polish boy going in that direction and smiled at him. He nodded back. Later my brother told me to stick to my own kind.

A couple of my birthdays passed in the pit, though there had been no cake or candles to celebrate. I measured time by how long it took the scar on my leg to fade, which was longer than expected because the leg kept getting reinfected. It looked like a pink balloon oozing with pus for a long time, and finally it became almost flat. That took about two years. Two of my best teenage years stolen by those Nazi rats. Two years in captivity, living in a pit underground with no birthdays, no celebrations whatsoever.

CHAPTER 12

Heidi

August 2023

Irene sits next to Mamaleh on the sofa as she reads from her tablet. "I am so sorry for the situation you had as a teenager," Irene says. "I feel very bad for what happened to you. May the Lord protect you from any more harm."

Mamaleh reaches for Irene's hand and nods.

"At least your parents were with you," Irene says. "My son is spending his teenage years in the Philippines with his grandparents, but that's not the same as living here with me. Thank the Lord, he's not underground in a pit like you were."

Mamaleh nods again in commiseration with Irene, whose facial features droop downward in sadness. Their heads tilt forward, barely touching, each lost in her own experience of grief. I'm not included in their tableau. My teenager years on Maple Drive were carefree. Safe. Not all that different from my life now.

"I've got to scoot," I say. "Jonathan—my nice pickleball coach—is meeting me at the courts."

"You're going to fall and break your hip with that pickleball *narishkeit*," Mamaleh warns. "Such foolishness. Getting a new hip at your age! It's no joke, my Heidi."

"Every sport has risks, you know, not just pickleball. You want me to chain myself to a bed and become a recluse? That would be much worse than playing, so stop worrying. See you tomorrow. Do you need anything?"

Before she has a chance to answer, I hike my pickleball bag onto my shoulder, happy to feel the familiar load, as if the bag filled with all my pickleball gear belongs just where it is. All these purchases—the court shoes, the paddle, the balls, the protective goggles—have become an extension of who I am. At the front door I turn and say thank you to Irene. Without her I'd be the caregiver stuck inside this house, though I could never live up to her standard of care.

Sprinting down Maple Drive toward the courts, I feel almost twenty-something again. The physical restrictions that I associated with being more than seventy years old are less daunting than I anticipated. Okay, I'm not zip-lining, scaling a mountain, or piloting a plane. But we boomers refuse to let age define us, right? All together now: You're only as old as you feel! Age is nothing but a number!

Until, that is, a cramp seizes my hamstring en route to my lesson with Jonathan. I'm struggling to straighten my knee when he sends me a text asking if we're still on for today. Is he kidding? I deserted my mother to meet him this afternoon. A little ache in the back of my leg is not going to stop me. Waving to him as I enter the park, I'm determined to make the session worthwhile. I won't tell him about my pulled hamstring, not to mention the stabbing pain in my arthritic right hip. He doesn't need to know.

Jonathan is standing near the net with a large basket of balls when I arrive. He's shorter than I recall from our previous lessons, but I was right about his compact body. He's strikingly fit for a guy in his sixties.

"Nice to see you," he says.

Staring into his mirrored sunglasses, I see my reflection. I'd prefer to peer into his unsheathed eyes, but that's a thought best kept to myself.

"Glad to be here." I tip the corners of my mouth up in a small smile.

"I thought Sylvia might be with you today. Have you heard from Syl?" He rotates his head in the direction of the street, obviously hoping to catch sight of her.

"No. She isn't answering my texts, but I can try again if you'd like."

"Maybe a bit later." His voice cracks. A worried gaze clouds his eyes. "Okay, then. Let's start."

Jonathan's initial dinks to me are disarmingly easy, but soon he is hitting topspin dinks, slice dinks, and cross-court dinks one after another, none of which I can return.

"Bend your knees," Jonathan instructs. "You can't play pickleball standing at attention like you're saluting a drill sergeant with your feet glued together. Get your paddle in ready position. It shouldn't be hanging at your side. Your feet should be shoulder-width apart and your knees slightly bent."

"Got it."

"And move your feet more. As I told you before, you need to shuffle to get those cross-court shots. Your weight should be on the balls of your feet. Chest up. Avoid using your lower back to get to the ball. And above all, don't backpedal to get the lobs over your head. Never run backward. You'll lose your balance, and then…"

My mind is churning with five things I should be doing and fifteen things I should not be doing. Sure, I know what to do. I just don't do what I know I'm supposed to be doing. I'm worried that I'll never be Jonathan's star pupil. He'll lose interest in me. Wait. He never was interested in me. What if I don't get an A+ on my pickleball report card? Oh, no worries. I forgot that in my high school, gym wasn't counted in my GPA.

After a few more lacklustre drills, Jonathan walks to my side of the court. "You seem distracted, Heidi," he says.

"Do I?"

"You know," he says, switching to a softer, more benevolent voice, "you don't need to try so hard. Your best performance will occur as soon as your mind is calm. A relaxed mind can concentrate and find ways to surpass limits."

"So when is that supposed to happen? In case you haven't noticed, I'm not getting any younger."

"It will happen when you're ready to experience just being here."

I want to hurl my paddle at Jonathan. What part of old age does this guy not get? Of course I'm distracted. My mother is processing painful wounds from her previous life, her caregiver is facing interminable separation from her son in the Philippines, and my friend Sylvia has taken up with some thug she met in the park. She won't even respond to my text messages. Who wouldn't be distracted?

"You're right, Jonathan," I say after a moment. "I am preoccupied. My mind is somewhere else. I apologize, but I'm worried about Sylvia. What if something terrible happened to her?"

"I'm worried too." He lifts his sunglasses, rests them on the top of his head, and dabs at the wetness collecting at the corners of his eyes. "Let's call it quits for today."

"If that's what you want." I don't need to be Sigmund Freud to see the panic transforming Jonathan's features, reshaping his expression into one of agonizing alarm. Somehow, I've underestimated the depth of his feeling for Sylvia. The truth is, I've tried hard not to see his unabashed desire for her, the sneak peeks at her breasts and remarks on her classy hair. Willful ignorance on my part. What else is new?

We pack up and leave the park. We don't speak again until Jonathan says goodbye at his car. The late-summer air warms my skin, but the euphoria I felt walking to the courts seems hidden now behind the clouds gathering in a foreboding sky.

CHAPTER 13

Sylvia

Two Years Earlier
2021

I may be off the mark on this, but it seems to me that the pandemic is already having a big impact inside families. At least inside my little family, and we're barely a year into this thing. With Danny working in his office downstairs and me being retired, it's hard to get much distance from each other. A separation sometimes would be useful, but where can I go? Danny's huge fear of contagion seems to give him licence to control my every move. He's so afraid of my exposure to the virus that I feel like a prisoner in my own house. Even getting together outside with my sister freaks him out.

One day last week at breakfast, I told Danny that my sister and I were going for a walk in the ravine. I don't speak to her often, so this was a big occasion for us. But I told Danny he didn't have to worry. We planned to follow the two-metre physical distancing guideline. Danny hit the roof. He stood up, took his plate of scrambled eggs and toast, which I had just made for him, and threw it into the sink. The plate broke. The eggs landed on the backsplash. "You're not going anywhere with that sister of yours." He scowled. "She's one of those anti-vaxxers who's perpetuating this epidemic and putting everyone at risk. And now you can clean up the mess." Which I did.

It's always possible that I'm exaggerating. His explosion wasn't that bad. (I've seen worse.) The kitchen looked spotless in twenty minutes. I called my sister to say that Danny lost his cool this morning, and I didn't want to aggravate him any further. As usual she advised me to get help. For the millionth time our conversation went like this:

Her: "You should set up a Zoom call with the rabbi or a counsellor at Jewish Family and Child Services."

Me: "Thanks, but no thanks."

I have no intention of bringing shame to the family. Being childless is more than enough. And I'm not going to destroy our marriage over Covid.

My sister doesn't get it. At my age, changing the situation isn't possible. The irony, of course, is that Danny doesn't see himself as controlling. From his perspective he's just a sensitive guy who likes to offer advice, wants to keep me safe, and doesn't like to be rebuffed. He also has a generous side, which sometimes manifests itself in gift giving. A while back he gave me a lovely orchid. It's thriving. I should know by now that he's easily frustrated, humiliated, and hurt. I always seem to let him down as a wife.

"Hey, Dan," I shout down to him in his office. "I'm going for a walk in the park on Maple Drive. By myself—so don't worry."

The park is almost empty when I get there. The play structures are wrapped in yellow caution tape to prevent children from catching the dreaded disease, but a few kids romp on the slide anyway. From the courts I hear a ball pinging and people shouting.

"Yours."

"Mine."

"Oops. Missed it. Sorry."

The closer I get, the more I sense their deep involvement in the game. Not one of them takes notice of me at the fence. My eyes follow the yellow ball back and forth until it stops, and the four players touch their paddles together.

"Looks like ping pong without a table," I say to one of the women who comes over to the bench for her water bottle. She's younger than I am, but not by much.

"No, it's pickleball. Great social outlet and a bit of exercise. Want to join us?"

"Not today. But are you always here?"

"Most days. You can get a paddle almost anywhere. Try Canadian Tire. A paddle won't cost more than seventy-five bucks there. Good enough for a beginner."

In the lonely world of Covid, that invitation felt tangible enough to carry me forward. I'd rather take a deep dive into the pickleball pandemic than my husband's coronavirus hysteria.

CHAPTER 14

Mamaleh

Recording 05.mp4

1944. A miracle happened one night in the underground cave where we hid. An unusual noise woke us. Mother complained that the stomping outside gave her a terrible headache. She couldn't possibly get a decent night's sleep with all that ruckus going on. Father told her to stop complaining because those boots she was hearing likely belonged to soldiers in the Soviet Union's Red Army who were marching into Poland to free us from the Nazis.

Through a crack in the earth, we watched the sky light up with fire from cannons somewhere near us. The clay walls began to crumble from the heavy strikes. But our family didn't care. We hoped to be returning home soon. Only Mother didn't want to go back to Szczniki and live among the dead. She said there would be too many whispering ghosts to haunt us.

Within days the Red Army drove the Nazis out of the area and hoisted a Soviet flag over the Polish landowner's barn. We survived! But the townspeople of Szczniki were shocked to see us alive because almost all the other Jews in our *shtetl* were rumoured to have perished. They stared at us suspiciously as my brother and I entered the town square. One guy wanted to know where our glamorous mother was. His buddies surrounded us. I recognized a couple of them from my father's tannery and the street corners where they used to taunt Mother.

"What happened to her fur coat? Ooh la la." They nudged each other and laughed.

"Yeah, Casimir. You must know who has those silver fox pelts. She used to wrap herself in fur down to her ankles. Remember, Casimir?"

The references to Mother made my mouth go dry. I stepped back, scared of the roughness in their voices. Maybe these guys planned to finish Hitler's work. My brother, Mendl, said nothing and tugged me away from them.

After those insults, I wondered why we returned to this place. Was it to reclaim our property? Impossible. Our house was nothing more than a pile of rubble. The cat's sandbox was still there, but what happened to our tabby cat, Challah? When I called out to him, he didn't come to see me. Maybe he'd found a different place to live, like we might be forced to do. I felt like a dinosaur facing extinction in the country of my birth and the land my ancestors had called home for generations. I vomited in the lane where I once skipped rope. Then we walked away.

CHAPTER 15

Heidi

August 2023

Tanya L. has organized a new Doubles session at Maple Drive Park on Friday, August 18 from 4:30 PM to 6:30 PM.

Click here to see details and join us.

Note: At the risk of stating the obvious, please remember that the Pickleball Organizer is not intended to be a court reservation system. We all know that we must follow the court rotation and sharing rules that apply to the courts on Maple Drive. Please show respect to others. Delete your name if your plans change. Don't play longer than the court rules allow.

I grab the only vacant spot, then remember I have an appointment with my ophthalmologist in the afternoon. Maybe she can tell me why the colour of the pickleball matters so much. We waste tons of time on the court deliberating about which colour ball to use. Some players swear by the orange balls, which they say they can see best; others prefer blue or bright pink. Many people can't see the yellow or green balls because there's too much glare and not enough contrast with the environment. The problem is aging eyes, I suspect. Is there any part of us that isn't in decline? I'm fine with any colour ball unless the plastic is cracked. Then the ball is a piece of junk headed for a landfill site or, hopefully, a recycling bin. But, as long as I can see, I intend to keep pounding that forty-hole round object against a paddle. It never fails to divert my attention from the ten other anxieties pressing on me.

Mamaleh's story is at the top of the list. Every aspect of it, no matter how small the detail, is painful to hear. I never knew she lost Challah. I didn't have an inkling that she owned or liked cats. In my childhood she abhorred furry four-legged creatures. If a stray cat pranced in front of us when we were strolling along Maple Drive, she grabbed my hand and pulled me in the opposite direction. No pets of any kind were allowed in our house, not even an innocent goldfish.

I glance at the names of the other players who are listed for the doubles session today. Tanya, Liz, Debbie, Arlene, and Sylvia signed up. Sylvia, really? I haven't heard from her since she walked off with that no-goodnik Joe. When I get to the courts about ten minutes late, Sylvia hasn't arrived yet. Tanya checks the Pickleball Organizer on her phone. There's a message from Sylvia:

Sorry can't make it. Next time. SG

At least she could have notified us earlier in the day that her plans changed. Oh, Sylvia. What's gotten into you? Disappointed, the group peppers me with questions about her, but I can't explain her erratic behaviour. I wish I could. In the past she was a reliable pickler, quiet, but happy to be one of us. In one of our first patio lunches, I remember Sylvia sitting between Debbie and Arlene, leaning forward, as if she wanted to share a secret with the group. She demonstrated a surprising interest in group gossip, given her penchant for numbers, accounting, and all things factual. Sylvia frequently posted messages on our WhatsApp chat, sharing news about the current trials and tribulations of group members. When Debbie fell backward and sprained her wrist on the court earlier in the summer, Sylvia was the first to let us know. And when Ron nearly lost his eye from a pickleball smacking his eye socket, Sylvia sent us a detailed message, quoting an ophthalmologist friend on the hazards of playing without eye protection.

Sylvia was diligent in sharing every shred of information she had to keep us safe. Health, safety, and the well-being of each of us were big concerns of hers. If one of the picklers was leaving for a vacation, Sylvia sent a WhatsApp message to that person saying, "Go in safety and return in safety." If a parent of a pickler died, Sylvia was the first to extend her condolences. Never careless or thoughtless, she obviously saw herself as a guardian in our emerging pickleball family. I can't fathom what happened to her.

When we begin to play, I'm not at my best. I send more balls into the net than I hit over it. "Oh shit, Heidi," I scold myself. "You stink today." I'm embarrassed by this performance. All the instructions Jonathan gave me rattle around in my head, but it's not Jonathan speaking the loudest to me. I'm the bossy one, giving myself the instructions, critical of my every move: Bend your knees more. Stay on the balls of your feet. Move. What kind of shot is that? I should have just blocked the ball. I'm wrecking the afternoon for everyone. Damn!

My self-talk is so intrusive that I'm unable to relax and concentrate. I offer to sit out the next game to refocus. Once on the bench, I realize I've had enough. As I pack up my shoes, I see Liz bend over to pick up something that has fallen behind the bench.

"Did anyone drop a hairband?" She holds up a thin, curved metal strip and waves it around. "Look what I found, guys. Who wants it?"

We're all wearing hats. The hairband doesn't belong to any of us. Besides, who would want it after it's been on the ground? It looks dirty and wet, as if it's been there for months.

"I'd throw it away," I say to Liz. "Nobody should touch that filthy thing." I take off my sunglasses and move closer to Liz to get a better view of the headband. "Wait a minute," I say. "That might be Sylvia's hairband. She has a pastel-blue one just like that. Same colour, same braided pattern."

She once told me that she bought it online from Simons. I always liked seeing her with the headband because it made her look like Alice in Wonderland. All she needed was a pinafore dress. But I'm surprised her hairband is on the ground. I wonder if she's playing here at times when we're not here? Or did she drop it as a clue? Maybe someone knocked it off her head.

"I'll text Sylvia to ask if it's hers," I say.

"Don't bother. Someone with Covid could have worn it or touched it," Tanya says. "Just leave that disgusting thing where it is."

"Maybe Sylvia can clean it up?" I suggest, thinking I should return the hairband to her. Isn't that what a big sister would do if she really cared about a fragile sibling who might be at risk?

Liz shrugs.

Sylvia doesn't respond to my text. Fuck this. I'm going to risk catching Covid and take it to her house. I hope she hasn't fallen down Alice's rabbit hole and entered a strange, alternate universe.

CHAPTER 16

Sylvia

One Year Earlier
June 2022

It began with a discussion about pickleball. Not really a discussion. More like a criticism. As I was leaving the house after lunch last Thursday to go to the courts, Danny said, "More pickleball. That's all you ever do."

I looked around the tidy kitchen, the fridge packed with food made from scratch, the family room festooned with freshly watered plants, the plush pillows on the sofa that I embroidered, the crumb-free carpet, the lamps with light bulbs that I had just changed, and said, "Pickleball is not all I ever do, but I see your point."

"It's a dangerous sport," he said. "You're too old to be playing. The chance of injury is very high."

Since when did Danny Greene show the slightest interest in my physical well-being? He typically caused the injuries rather than prevented them, but that was a conversation for another day when I wasn't pressed for time. With as much restraint as I could muster, I replied, "Life is dangerous. If I get injured, I'll heal."

"Not so fast," Danny said in an obvious effort to extend the discussion and delay my departure. "I looked on the internet," he continued. "The most common injuries are falls, shoulder sprains, elbow tendinitis, calf and hamstring strains, wrist fractures, rolling an ankle, twisting a knee, tearing a ligament. The recovery time on these injuries isn't a couple of days. We can be talking months. Sometimes surgery's required."

"Are you trying to scare me out of playing?" I was fed up with Danny's ridiculous terror tactics. All I wanted was to get away from him. "If so, stop. I don't need the fear of God following me onto the pickleball court."

"Just so you know, injuries are far more likely to occur in players who are fifty and over. Don't expect me to take care of you if you're clumsy enough at your age to hurt yourself."

Of course he would play the age card. "Don't worry," I assure him. "I'm warming up before I play. Besides, the benefits of playing far outweigh the risks, like moving, having fun, being part of a community."

"Your head is filled with such crap, Sylvia. It's too dangerous, and I don't want you to keep playing. I forbid it."

"But," I said, beginning to panic about the direction this conversation was going, "I like being part of the group. It keeps me busy and active. I see real faces that aren't in one of those little Zoom squares on a screen. I hear grunts and laughter. We're alive. We can live without being mediated by electronics. Imagine that. No Zoom. Hurrah!"

"You wouldn't have so much time on your hands if you had kids and grandkids, like everybody else."

"Sorry about that, Danny. But what's the point of rehashing that again? Infertility is what it is. We both know that."

"Stop playing that idiotic pickle game," he warned. "I'm telling you. You're going to end up in a rehab ward somewhere by yourself because you'll have nobody to care for you."

"You can threaten me all you want, but I'm playing anyway."

For the second time I tried to leave the house. That time I succeeded despite Danny's harangue, which was to be expected, I guess.

That little tiff between Danny and me a week ago has become our daily ritual. After we rehashed the whole thing again today and just before my pickleball escape, I put a plant on the windowsill—not my orchid, it's too sunny for it to flourish there—where I can watch it sprout leaves and eventually bend toward the light. From the window I love to see my garden blooming with my late-summer lilies and dahlias. Danny never understood why I started a flower garden in our backyard. The patch of land at the front of our house is a complete disaster, but Danny insists that it remain that way. He likes to give the impression that we're penniless, so burglars won't be tempted to rob us. If he's worried about a break-in, a security system would be a better option, if you ask me. (He never does ask me.) Our friends aren't interested in visiting us in this depressing mess of a place either. Danny doesn't mind that. Even before Covid, he loathed the idea of having people to dinner at our house. Whenever I complain that we're hermits, he yells that we're not hermits, and I should stop behaving like a drama queen. I fear that if he ever has a knife in his hand, he'll stab me.

Anything to get me to shut up and stop challenging him.

While I water my plant on the windowsill, Danny comes up behind me and puts his arms around my waist and nestles the top of his head into my neck and says, "I do love you, baby, you know that, don't you?"

It would be a nice moment if I didn't have a pickleball game scheduled. I never want to disappoint the pickleball gang. Besides, I like being reliable. I rarely missed a day at the office in all my thirty-five years of work. I'm always on time, on schedule. You can set a clock by me.

I leave the lunch dishes in the sink, knowing the mess will be there when I get back, and zip over to the courts. A silly jingle pops into my head as I skip along: *Too bad, Danny, you can't wreck my fun. So sad, Danny, the game is never done.* Have I ever really bonded with Dan Greene, I wonder, or do I simply feel shackled to him? I don't know how I saddled myself with this man and this marriage. No, not saddled. Wrong word. I love Danny. I really do. And he can be generous when he wants to be.

I pick up the pace as I turn down Maple Drive. I want to play the first game, which starts in just a few minutes.

CHAPTER 17

Heidi

August 2023

Sylvia's blue braided hairband rests in my hand. Once lovely, it's now wet and dirty, but hopefully not beyond repair. Maybe a handy person could polish it and make it look new again if Sylvia doesn't want to try herself. Or she could order a new one from Simons. Actually, I feel that finding the headband is some sort of an omen. Now I have an excuse to visit Sylvia at home. It's been too long since we've heard from her. She's disappeared. And I miss not seeing her regularly, not talking, not playing together. I miss the burst of pleasure that comes with making a friend late in life and bonding with that person, as if you've grown up together. More common in older age is the painful loss of dear friends. I squeeze Sylvia's soiled hairband to hold on to her.

Still, I hesitate to visit her house, uninvited and alone, but I have no choice. The other pickleball players are always busy with one thing or another. Besides, giving the hairband back is my job because I know her the best, although that's not saying much. She's so secretive about her life off the court. Most pickleball players that I know share all sorts of stories about their spouses, kids, grandkids, siblings, and aging parents between games. But not Sylvia. She's extremely reserved about her personal affairs.

So what. I won't allow her reticence to put me off. The hairband is hers, after all, and I'd like to see Sylvia to make sure she's okay. I drive up Maple Drive and turn left, just the way I did that rainy day, which now seems so long ago. About a block and a half south, I arrive at her house, a yellow brick, set far back from the road. Tall, untamed shrubs block a clear vision of the front door. Dense, wild foliage of different heights and textures takes the place of a manicured lawn. I'm guessing that the aim was to create an uncontrolled, natural English garden landscape, which can be wondrous, but hardly reflects Sylvia's orderly style. I hadn't noticed how dreary or secluded the house looked when I dropped her off in the rain.

I park in the driveway behind the car that's already there. I don't think it's Sylvia's car. I'm not even sure she knows how to drive because she always walks to the courts. As I make my way toward her house, I notice that the white trim around the windows and door, as well as the white railing, is chipped and dirty. It's hard to believe that Sylvia lives here.

A man answers when I ring the bell. I assume he's her husband, but his beard is so scruffy that I can't tell how old he is. The stoop in his posture suggests he's in his midsixties, close to Sylvia's age. He doesn't open the storm door, and through the screen I see a ragged hole in the elbow of his shirt sleeve. Diminished ability to care for himself or what?

"Hi there, I'm Heidi, one of Sylvia's pickleball friends," I say, trying to sound cheery despite my growing concern for Sylvia's well-being in a place like this. "I assume you're Sylvia's husband, yes?"

"I am her husband, yes. Can I help you?"

"Nice to meet you," I say, then plunge ahead with my reason for coming. "We found this hairband on the court today. I'm pretty sure it's Sylvia's. She told me she bought it online from Simons. Is she home? I'd like to give it back to her. I know how much she really likes it." I watch his face for a reaction, studying his eyes for some sign of affection for Sylvia. If he cares about her, he's not showing it.

"Thanks. I don't recognize the hairband, but I'll take it and ask her about it later. She's not home now." He opens the outer door a crack and reaches for it.

"No, no. I'd like to keep it until I see her." I withdraw the hairband and hold it down at my side. "No worries. I'll clean it up for her so she can wear it again. Anyway, tell her hi from me."

"Your name again is…?"

"Heidi. Heidi Allen." To delay my departure, I make small talk while taking advantage of the opportunity to put in a good word for Sylvia. "You know, your wife is a great pickleball player. Much better than I am, and she's very serious about improving her game."

"Yes, she plays often, doesn't she? Look, Miss Allen, I'm very busy with work. I'm expecting a call shortly. I must say goodbye."

"Sorry to disturb you. Just tell Sylvia hello from all of us. We miss her at the courts."

He closes the door and locks it. I turn away from the house, disappointed that I didn't get to see Sylvia. As I walk toward my car, I glance over my shoulder and look up at the second-floor windows. I see an oblong window draped in heavy dark fabric; an octagonal window in the middle of the house, which is most likely the bathroom; and on the far side of the house, I notice a large picture window covered in gauzy white curtains. Behind the curtain I detect a blur, a shadow of a person, maybe a female figure, judging from the silhouette of the person's hair, though I can't be sure. I wave, but suddenly the shadowy figure vanishes. This apparition must be a figment of my imagination, I tell myself. It can't be Sylvia. Her husband said she's not home. Wherever Sylvia is, she's probably fine.

No. After this visit, I don't believe Sylvia is fine. Her husband's behaviour seems particularly dodgy to me. Nor did the shambolic state of the exterior of their house inspire confidence in Sylvia's mental and physical health. It's just a hunch on my part, but I wouldn't be surprised if her existence is under some sort of threat. I should be taking action to rescue her. Either I'm a coward or a bad friend, or both.

CHAPTER 18

Mamaleh

How can I not tell you this? *Ach*! I'm *verklempt* just remembering what happened. You know how choked up I can get.

Recording 06.mp4

1945. In Szczniki, when my brother Mendl and I walked away from the rubble that used to be our home, we were even more determined to check on our grandparents' house nearby. When we got there we asked each other, is this it? Someone had replaced Grandma Ruth's brocade drapes with gaudy red velvet ones. A mangy mutt missing half an ear prowled at the gate. A German shepherd sitting on his haunches, ready to pounce, guarded the front door. When the mutt came over to me and tried to sniff my crotch, I jumped aside. Whoever was living here wanted to keep visitors away, especially visitors who were the legitimate homeowners and not visitors at all.

We slunk around to the back of the house and peeked through the window in the kitchen, where a woman was placing a pot on the stove. I raised my fist to knock on the glass and frighten her by making a ghoulish face with bulging eyes and a crooked smile, but my brother yanked me away. I felt rage. How did this woman have the nerve to use Bubbie's favourite cast iron pot? What if she boiled beef in cow's milk or steamed shellfish in it? Grandma would flip if she saw what was going on in her kosher kitchen. At the far end of the garden, a man roasted a pig on a spit. The sizzling pork fat dripped onto the grass. Disgusted, we left to explore the town for familiar landmarks.

The more I saw of Szczniki, the more I felt like a stranger. My mother was right. Returning Jews were considered intruders in our hometown, phantoms from a past that the townspeople didn't want to revisit. But I wasn't ready to give up.

On the window of our grandparents' photography studio, where the name of their shop used to be, I read "Fotografia" written in a different, fancier script. Underneath, the new owner had painted his name in the same frilly script: "Jan Rzemuwski." He had removed the Schreiber name and Grandma's tinted portraits of elderly Mr. Plotkin and the Kornblums holding plump baby Josef. Scenes of the Tatra Mountains now graced the studio windows, retouched with coloured inks so they resembled painted landscapes. Rzemuwski's photos were beautiful for what they were, I admitted, and sad for what they were not. I was so disappointed that my grandmother's photos were not where they should be that my stomach heaved violently without bringing anything up. We knocked on the door. When no one answered, I tested the handle.

The man who opened the door didn't invite us in. He stood in front of us, blockish in body, like a human barricade. A cigarette dangled from the corner of his mouth, and his arms were wrapped across his chest. Did he know what had happened to all the photos left in the Schreiber Studio of Photography, we asked. Had he found the bushels of negatives stored upstairs in our grandfather's photo processing lab? No, he assured us. The building was empty when he moved to Szczniki from Lviv. He took the last few puffs on his cigarette, then flicked the butt onto the street.

As we walked away from the studio, streaks of burnt orange and gold shimmered in the late afternoon sky. Shopkeepers I didn't recognize began to shutter their windows, and pedestrians failed to nod when they passed us on the street.

Despite the town's cold reception, Father was determined to resume our lives here. Within the span of a month or two, he removed the trespassers from Bubbie and Zaydie's house, purified every dirty pot, and then invited the few other Jewish survivors from Szczniki to live with us. Three weddings took place under our roof on a single night. A photographer could not be found to take official pictures. What a blessing that was. The couples wore clothes that would have appalled my grandmother, who was a portrait photographer and always aimed to capture the tasteful respectability of her clients. One bride found a rose-coloured blouse still hanging in Bubbie's closet and put it on backward after she popped off the buttons trying to fasten them. It was all a little strange, I thought, smiling at the bride in the backward blouse.

Everything about returning to Szczniki seemed backward. Strangeness felt like the norm.

Even when the underground Polish Home Army and the occupying Russian troops disturbed our sleep with their skirmishes, that seemed normal too.

One night after a big meal, the guests stayed around the table recounting their wartime stories. Outside, the sound of grenades surprised none of us. The gunfire wasn't loud enough or close enough to make us feel alarmed. I wished the noise would stop soon so we could have a good sleep. In the bedroom that my brother Mendl and I shared, we undressed and went to separate sides of our single mattress. Moments later a rock flew through the open window and hit the floor. Mendl hustled me out of the bedroom and up the staircase to find our parents. Not more than a minute after we ran away from that space, a bomb landed on our bed and exploded. I looked over my shoulder to see a cloud of feathers from the comforter floating up to the ceiling.

A gang of local thugs rampaged through the house, like a reign of terror, smashing wardrobes and overturning tables. The guests staying in our grandparents' house with us escaped by jumping from the second-floor windows. Some locked themselves into the outdoor toilet. But when Father insisted that we do the same, Mother refused. She told us to hide inside the house in the attic. We rushed upstairs to the closet at the far corner of a large storage area. Father pulled a chest of drawers in front of the closet to conceal our hiding place, lightly scraping the floor with the chest's claw feet. The door was open just enough for us to crawl inside. Father jammed himself into the lowest part of the closet where the sloping roof of the house met the attic floor. He lay there with Mendl flat on top of him. Mother sat at the front of the closet facing the door. I squeezed behind her. My arms circled her waist; my chest pressed into the curve of her back. With our positions fixed, she inched the door closed.

Sometime past midnight, boots struck the stairs leading to the attic. I heard a gruff voice say that she probably hid her silver fox coat in a closet up here in the attic. Ask Casimir, one of the thugs ordered when they were near the top of the steps. Casimir would be the one to know. He knew Miriam, really knew her. They all laughed.

Two minutes later I heard them in the attic, gasping for breath. When one guy pointed out the scratch on the floor, he shoved the chest of drawers off to the side of the attic door and turned the door handle. It fell off and dropped on the floor.

I muffled a cry by pressing my mouth into my mother's neck. Father reached forward and patted my shoulder to hush my sobbing. The attic closet was so dark that I couldn't figure out where the walls or the door were. When I let go of Mother for a moment to stretch my arms, I felt a damp surface to the left and right. My finger touched something sticky, like a spider's web. The cold walls felt as if they had been built hundreds of years ago, and no light had fallen in that space since. I leaned my head against Mother's back. I held on to her and stayed like that for a while, feeling the heat of her body until I felt her move forward and detach herself from me.

Father pushed her toward the door. "Go," he whispered. "Beg."

I pulled on her waist to hold her back, but she crawled out of the closet and tapped the door shut with her heel. When they asked her where the coat was, she said she didn't know. "Liar!" they yelled and sprayed bullets on the walls surrounding the closet, just missing my father, brother and me, holed up inside.

I listened to another round of flying bullets, counting the booms—four, five, six—while I huddled in the dark. Eight, nine... When the shots stopped, I wondered if she was alive. Maybe the bullets had missed her, and on the other side of the door, Mother would still be breathing.

The thugs fled down the stairs. For a few seconds, no air moved in or out of my lungs. Nobody spoke. Father, Mendl, and I remained in the closet, too terrified to move, in case someone had stayed behind. When we heard nothing—not even a groan or a whimper from her—Father broke the stillness. We crawled out of the closet. She lay in a puddle of blood. He pronounced her dead.

CHAPTER 19

Heidi

September 2023

Her reading hits me with the force of a tsunami and sucks me into a whirlpool of sadness. I'm overwhelmed thinking about the attic closet, my mother curled around her mother's back, holding in her scared little sobs, then a second later hearing the rat-a-tat-tat of the bullets which took away the grandmother I would never know. I sink to the floor near the sofa where Mamaleh is sitting. Her memories arouse fury in me, but also fear. Could a brutal murder like that someday remove another member from our family, one of my sons or grandkids? I'd like to return to the scene of my grandmother's murder, to see the place for myself, to experience what Mamaleh felt so that my lost Bubbie would also belong to me.

"Why didn't you tell me about your mother's death in the attic sooner?" I ask Mamaleh. "You never divulged anything about her." That's not exactly true. I do know that I supposedly look like her, but what did she look like? I've never seen a photo of her.

Mamaleh says nothing. Irene gives me a disapproving frown.

I question Mamaleh again. "How is it possible that you never mentioned the attic in all these years?" I'm baffled by her long silence, which shut me out of my own history, as if I were a stranger in my family's story. "Were you ever planning to inform me of anything that happened back then?"

Mamaleh still says nothing. Her eyes are closed. Irene sits nearby, holding her hand. She shakes her head. "Let Mommy rest in peace. Whatever the reason, don't challenge her now."

When I arrive at the pickleball courts in the afternoon, I am still processing the brutal murder of my grandmother and my mother's decision to keep it a secret. If it had not been for Covid and the time we dedicated to video-recording her tablet, Mamaleh would never have revealed how my grandmother died.

"Hey, Heidi. You don't look so great today," Lisa says as we take our places at the baseline of the court, our pickleball paddles in ready position. "Is it a migraine or something else?"

"I wish it were only a migraine. Tell you later." My grandmother's violent end torments me during the entire game, like a punch in the face followed by a body slam.

"What ails you today?" Lisa says after the game. I'm ready to collapse and be carried home. When I give her the short version, she says, "My father is a survivor too. He always told me to never let your enemies stop you from living freely and without fear."

"Fear," I say, raising an eyebrow. "I could write a book about fear."

"Why don't you?" Lisa appears to be seventy-five percent teasing and twenty-five percent serious. "You've convinced me. You're an expert."

"Thanks for your vote of confidence, Lisa. At least I'm good at something. My top fear at this moment is more about the present than the past. Whenever I play pickleball on Maple Drive, I worry about what happened to Sylvia. I tried to return her hairband, but her husband nearly lopped off my nose when he shut the door in my face. I bet he wouldn't do that to a strapping guy like our coach, Jonathan. I'm afraid for her."

"I agree. Something's wrong," Lisa says. "People don't vanish the way Sylvia did. Poof! And she disappeared."

"Yup." I'm shaking. I gulp the water remaining in my bottle, but it doesn't quench my thirst or quell my fears. Call me an obsessively fearful worrywart, but I can't stop my brain from dwelling on Sylvia.

CHAPTER 20

Jonathan

September 2023

When Heidi contacts me about a pickleball lesson, I hesitate to respond. It's unlike me to behave like a complete shmuck, but here's the thing. The last time I arranged a lesson with Heidi, she was too damn distracted to focus on the game. Her life seemed to be spinning out of control, but the warning signs slipped past me. Come to think of it, I'm not sure Heidi herself gave me too many clues. No tears. No explosions—except when she freaked out over Sylvia's behaviour with those thugs in the park. That scared the shit out of me too. What was that all about? Totally off the wall if you ask me. Syl is such a class act. The streaked blonde hair held back with a hairband. A kind of Grace Kelly elegance. The understated clothes. Nothing flashy or wild about her. I should have grabbed her arm and pulled her away from those punks that night. Something had already starting to jell between us. I tried, but failed. My super bad.

I text Heidi that I'm very, very busy and unavailable for a lesson in the next few weeks, but she doesn't take no for an answer. A few days later she messages me again:

Jonathan, pretty please, can you find an hour in your super busy schedule when we can play. Pickleball is just what I need now. Something hopeful, fun.

I'm at the club when I read her message. The club is my happy place—eager clients saying hi, the thumping of the ball against many paddles, people of all ages joking about their pathetic swings. These sounds are music to my ears. I love being the pro, the expert, the fixer, inundated with requests for advice on how to play the game. Okay. What the hell. I'll meet with Heidi. No skin off my back. Maybe she has info about Sylvia. I text back:

I have cancellation tomorrow. Meet me at Maple Drive courts 7:30 a.m. 30 minutes max

She appears in the park right on time, wide awake and raring to go in a sleeveless top and tights. I'm stunned by her bouncy energy, her quick change into court shoes, her calf stretches and shoulder rolls before the lesson begins. I'm exhausted just watching her.

"Hey, Heidi, how old are you, if you don't mind me asking?" We're dinking the ball across the net to each other, and she hasn't missed one.

"I'm seventy-three, just months away from my next birthday." She bends her knees to scoop a low ball at her feet.

"Wow! You don't look it."

"This is what seventy-three looks like." She appears indignant rather than pleased by the compliment. "Stop being ageist, Jonathan, and let's get started."

I sure didn't see that coming. Sylvia would never be so confrontational. In fact, I'm willing to bet she'd sew her mouth shut to avoid any possibility of a clash. While we're dinking, I ask Heidi if she's heard from her. The corners of Heidi's mouth tug downward for the first time this morning.

"Nope." She suddenly looks like she's edging toward a cliff and the fall below will break her bones. I don't know if she's worried about

Sylvia—I am—or if she's upset about something I said. Women never cease to perplex me.

When we move from drills to a game of skinny singles on half court, Heidi misses two out of every three shots I hit to her. And that's when her negativity really kicks in to high gear. She swears like a sailor and dwells on her mistakes. Missed opportunities are cause for an outpouring of self-doubt.

"You should have had that easy one, asshole. Heidi, you're a fucking loser." That's not me talking. She's ragging on herself.

"Okay. Time out." We walk to the bench and sit at opposite ends with our gear between us. "It's not your shots that I'm concerned about, Heidi. It's your critical self-talk. You don't seem to trust yourself to play a smart game."

"That's not true," she says. "Of course I do. I trust myself enough to get here, to hire you as a coach. That shows trust."

"No, that shows commitment," I tell her. "You can show up. You can practice and work hard. But you haven't made the next step of trusting your brain and your body to execute the right shots."

"Bullshit. I want to play, and I'm putting in the effort to get better." She squints and flashes an accusing look my way.

No worries, I tell myself. I'm used to this kind of resistance. Comes with the territory. "I know you're committed to the game, Heidi, but you don't have the right mental attitude to take it to the next level. I suspect you're one of those perfectionists who lets a mistake destroy you, whether the error has any impact on the endgame or not. Sorry, but that's what I see happening on the court."

"Fuck off, Jonathan. Basically, you don't believe an old dog can learn new tricks," she rants at me. "You like to spout niceties about human potential and acorns turning into magnificent oak trees, but really, you're guilty of the worst kind of hypocritical ageism imaginable. And you're patronizing me with this 'trust yourself' bullshit. If you really believe I have potential, you'd be coaching me about getting my paddle in the right position for each shot. You'd be telling me which shot I should be making every time. You'd be advising me to punish my opponent's mistakes (not that I have the chutzpah to punish a flea). But you're not doing any of those things because, let's face it, Jonathan, you don't really believe that old people have the potential to excel in this sport or any sport."

"That's a fucking lie and you know it," I protest. "Just calm down, Heidi." I'm embarrassed that a couple of players on the other courts are glaring at her losing it.

"Look, Jonathan," she rails, "you basically believe that seniors are in a state of decline, and it's downhill all the way from here. Sure, our ability to see the ball is diminishing. Our fast twitch muscles aren't twitching so fast anymore—if they ever did. We're tippy and prone to falls. That's what you really think, isn't it? I see the disdain in your eyes and that condescending smile of yours. It makes me sick. And I don't want to calm down!"

As the words fly angrily off her tongue, hot and bitter, I can almost believe them. I am almost convinced that there is an ageist tendency in my coaching style, though unintentional, of course. I'm beginning to appreciate Heidi for pointing out my flaws. I'm making a mental note to work on changing my attitude when she turns toward me and whips an orange pickleball in my direction, hitting me on the mouth.

"Whoa, Heidi. Cool it." There's no point trying to refute, or even agree with, her accusations when she's this upset. Right now she won't be able to hear my promise to improve my coaching. "You nearly knocked out one of my teeth."

"Sorry, Jonathan. I didn't intend to hit you. I just lost control. That was terrible of me. Anyway, I'm out of here," she huffs. "I'll e-transfer the fifty bucks to you for today's partial lesson. Keep the change and have a great day."

"It's no big deal, Heidi. Don't bother." Only when I arrive home do I look more closely in a mirror and notice that my front teeth are slightly pink. There's a film of blood at the gumline where Heidi's pickleball smacked my mouth. An occupational hazard, I suppose, in an otherwise nonviolent sport—until it isn't. Maybe I need a mouth guard in addition to protective goggles.

After twenty-four hours with no message from Heidi, I figure we're finished. She's got her truth, and she's sticking to it. But then I get an apologetic text from her asking me to forgive her for the outburst and for throwing a ball at me. She was upset about Sylvia. Who isn't? She pleads with me to go to Sylvia's house. I should try to speak to her and find out what's going on. It's a desperate situation, Heidi writes. Please do something fast.

I don't want to get into the middle of this mess with Sylvia. I typically shy away from any involvement with clients. It's not kosher. I'm a strong believer in keeping my work and personal lives separate. (Ha! Who am I kidding? I've had my share of trysts with younger and older clients, some more serious than others. Full transparency has never been my M.O.) If Heidi were asking me to rescue anyone else, I'd beg off, but I can't abandon Syl after what's happened between us.

I text Heidi to ask for Sylvia's address. In return Heidi sends me an abundance of information and orders—enough to have carried out the kidnapping of John Paul Getty III. She describes the exterior of Sylvia's two-storey yellow brick hidden behind a tangle of bushes. The address is 57 Shoremount, several blocks southwest of Maple Drive. If her husband answers the door, I should tell him I have a gift for Sylvia from her pickleball friends because we haven't seen her for a while and we're wondering what happened to her. I should bring Sylvia a box of candy—it must be dark-chocolate almond bark—with a bow on top. I should make the delivery today.

Will do, I message Heidi, though what makes her think this ruse will work? I doubt that Sylvia's husband will greet me any more graciously than he greeted Heidi. Why would he, unless I produce a search warrant or use some cheap gimmick to fool him?

Three days later, after several pestering texts from Heidi, I ring the bell at 57 Shoremount, pretending to be a courier with a package for Sylvia Greene. The front garden is so overgrown that you'd need a machete to clear it. Heidi warned me of that. Yet I'm still surprised, given how neat and tidy Sylvia is. How does she live here, I wonder. Maybe she doesn't.

I'm wearing grey dress pants, a blue button-down shirt, and a jacket that has a courier company's logo on it, borrowed at the last minute from one of my clients at the club who moonlights as a courier.

Sylvia's husband, looking like an irritable slob, answers after several rings. If he ever had muscles, they've turned to flab. His glasses sit on the tip of his nose, which forces him to tilt his chin down and raise his eyebrows to make eye contact with me. I detect a whiff of body odour as a breeze shifts his nasty smell toward me. He reaches out to take the package.

"Sir, this is for Sylvia Greene. Is she here to sign for it?"

"I'm her husband. I'll take it." He looks over my shoulder, checking out my car in the driveway.

"Sir, I'm afraid there's a request for her signature on delivery." I point to the packing slip on the box. "I've got strict instructions that the recipient whose name is on the package must sign for it."

"Look, I'm her husband, Daniel Greene. I can sign for it."

"I'm sorry, sir. I could lose my job if you forge her signature."

He tries to shut the door, but not before I plant my shoe in the middle of the doorsill. I've borrowed steel-toed boots from another client for this encounter, but his feet are a half size smaller than mine. Squished toes and Daniel Greene's hostility bring my patience to a boiling point.

"Now you look here, sir," I say. "I need to see your wife to obtain her signature. As I said, those are the rules. When will she be back? If necessary, I can deliver the package another day."

"If you step foot on this property again, I'll call the police." He tries to shove me away from the door, but I step back before he closes it.

I walk down the steps with the package undelivered. On the bottom step I hear a tap-tap on one of the second-floor windows.

I glance up. I can't see a person there, but what if Syl is hiding behind the curtains. Every nuance of expression I've ever seen on her face comes back to me. The way her smile slides slowly into place. The scrunch of her nose when she dislikes something. Then there's another tap-tap.

CHAPTER 21

Sylvia

September 2023

My knuckles hit the window with short, sharp blows. Then I quickly step back before Jonathan sees me. I should have smashed my fist through the pane of glass and yelled for help. I should have, but I didn't. What if the shattering glass hit Jonathan and blinded him? What if Danny heard me scream? What if the sound of the breaking window infuriated him? He might have rushed upstairs, burst into this room, and choked me. His unpredictable violence is a possibility I always live with. I can't separate my fear of him from the love I still feel. My hand goes limp. I close my eyes. Even if I wanted to scream, I can't. Because part of me believes that I deserve to be locked up in here. I'm not sure how long I've been confined to this room. I only know that my confinement began in late August when I returned from the drug drop-off downtown.

Danny had suspected wrongdoing on my part the minute I walked through the front door. Honestly, he should have been a detective instead of an engineer. We know each other so intimately that any inconsistency in my behaviour arouses his suspicion.

"Where did you get that sweatshirt?" he had asked. His eyes scrolled up and down my body, like he was hunting for a specific word on a page in the *Oxford English Dictionary* and found it. "Atrocious! It looks disgusting on you. Not your style."

"I bought it at Winners. I took the bus there this afternoon." I looked directly at him and held his gaze, trying to disguise my shame.

"Really? How much did it cost?" The jeering tone of his voice shook me. Had he already figured out that I was mired in a lie?

"Not much," I said, smiling. "I got a deal. It was on sale for about twenty-five dollars. Here's the money if you want it." I reached into my purse to find the bills Joe had just given me.

"No, no. Show me the receipt. I want evidence that you were where you said you were."

"Of course." I rifled through my purse and the pockets of the sweatshirt. "Sorry, I've lost the receipt."

"You're lying to me. You never lose a receipt or misplace anything, Sylvia. You've got the fastidious, detailed mind of an accountant."

We were still in the living room. A pale light streamed through the blinds, signalling that dinnertime was fast approaching. I tried to walk around Danny to reach the kitchen, but he pivoted and grabbed me by the arm. I flung my hand against his chest, trying to push him away, but I couldn't make him let go. He manoeuvred my arm behind my back and twisted it with so much force that I could barely lift it when he finally let it drop. I feared he'd dislocated my shoulder. *Adios*, pickleball, I thought. I'm out for at least a month.

I did my best to cook a one-handed meal—not my most stellar dinner, to be sure—while Danny paced from one room to another, occasionally mumbling, "You're lying to me, you little whore."

Over dinner I lowered my eyes. "Danny, I've made a terrible mistake." I should have known that this was the wrong time to confess my true whereabouts that afternoon. His mood was already foul. But I wanted to be honest with him, to try to establish trust between us.

"What kind of terrible mistake?" His voiced sounded strained. He searched my face for clues.

I couldn't look at him. "I was involved in a drug deal." I put the phone that Joe gave me on the table. I never wanted to hear from him again. "If you want evidence, here it is."

He pushed away from the table, rocking the serving dish of pasta on its side. A half-full bottle of Perrier tipped over and rolled onto the floor.

I jumped up to get the mop. "Wait, Danny. It's not as bad as you think. I'm done with drug trafficking. It's over now, completely over. No more lies. I won't do anything horrible like that again."

Later that night, he confiscated my computer and cell phone. When I protested, he dragged me into my study and locked the door, cutting me off from the outside world. He nailed the window shut. I became a prisoner in my own house.

Now, waiting for Danny to deliver dinner feels interminable. I watch the sun set to estimate the time of day. By my reckoning, at least an hour remains before a skimpy meal of canned soup and rice arrives. All I can think about is how I allowed myself to become involved with this unbalanced man. I rehash the details of our meeting, but the more I go over that night and the decades that followed, the less sense any of it makes.

I was so young when it all began, just graduating from high school. I met him at a cousin's bat mitzvah party. Nearly everyone I knew was jealous of me because Danny Greene was an older, grounded sort of guy. He had a car and lived in Forest Hill. But coming from Forest Hill didn't make Danny Greene into a *mensch*. He attended the University of Toronto, like lots of kids from Toronto did, lived at home, majored in engineering, and fit the stereotype of a geeky engineer to a tee. Back then, I thought of engineers as hugely practical guys in a field that was dominated by men. I assumed that Danny would be a walking encyclopedia when it came to how to fix houses and cars. Of course we'd live in Forest Hill. I imagined us in one of those sprawling mansions on Warren Road. A double lot for rows of flowers if I got lucky. That was my naïve fantasy of our life together. And in the beginning the future did look rosy. I entered the University of Toronto with the dream of going straight through to a PhD in mathematics. I had ambitions—I was determined to make a significant contribution to the world's knowledge of chaos theory. Danny and I married young, when I was in the first year of my master's degree in the Department of Mathematics. Elated, I believed I was right on track for a solid academic career.

Danny, however, saw my destiny differently. He complained that I was obsessed with math stardom. (Me, a star. Ridiculous!) He grumbled that my intense focus on studying and my obsessive drive to complete the graduate degree program prevented me from concentrating on starting a family. (More ridiculous!) Why didn't I do something practical rather than theoretical, he argued. Soon he began to pester me to apply for teaching positions in math at a community college or a local high school. I'd have summers off, he would tell me, and I could contribute a steady income to our household. Why, oh why, did I listen to him? I still can't answer that, but I took his advice, like an obedient wife. That was what women did back then. When the opportunity arose to teach a couple of math courses at George Brown College, which was only a bus ride away from where we lived, I took the job and put the completion of my master's degree on hold. I was convinced I'd come back to it, then go on to do a PhD in math. Maybe not right away—maybe not for years—but in the back of my mind, it was still the way I defined myself: an academic mathematician currently on a break.

Instead, the George Brown School of Business advertised a full-time position in their accounting program. I was sweet and reliable with a foot already in the door. Little wonder that I was hired for the job. I never went back to U of T, nor did I remain an instructor at George Brown College. After I'd taught for several semesters, Danny once again criticized the amount of time and energy I devoted to my work. Again, he perceived my busy career as an obstacle to becoming pregnant. (Stupendously ridiculous!) To avoid his constant nagging, I quit teaching and accepted a nine-to-five support position in a small accounting firm, where I stayed until I retired thirty-five years later.

When I hear Danny unlock the door to my study with a tray of food, my mood lifts. That is, until he warns me that if my friends come to the front door again, there will be consequences.

Consequences for them or me, I wonder. Has he forgotten that I have no way to contact them? I know he detests interruptions and distractions when he's working, but I'm the powerless one in this scenario. He can make change happen, but I can't. Engineers are presumably problem solvers and thinkers by default. So solve the problem already, Danny, while hope still glimmers.

CHAPTER 22

Heidi

September 2023

How awful that Jonathan made zero progress with Sylvia's husband. If he is her gatekeeper, this guy is doing a hell of a job at it. Neither Jonathan nor I can force her husband to release information about Sylvia's whereabouts. If she's at home, he's determined to keep that a secret too. What a gruff bastard he is. Just imagining Sylvia locked in that shambolic house on Shoremount with her monster husband terrifies me.

For what it's worth, I still have her tarnished blue hairband, somewhat cleaner after I spent forty-five minutes trying to remove dirt from the crevices in the braided pattern. I'll admit it doesn't look as good as new. But I know she's touched it, worn it, pulled back her streaked hair with it. That's enough of a memento for me. Running my fingers along the metal band, I feel more compelled to free Sylvia. My thoughts return to the moment when one of the picklers—Liz, I think—found the hairband behind the court bench. She wanted to throw it away. But now the curved piece of metal feels like a precious object, and the courts on Maple Drive have become a sacred space. I first met Sylvia there. She often sat on the bench exactly where we discovered her lost hairband. She chatted with us. We grew to be friends. We weathered a storm together just up the street. Now I fear that the bench and her hairband may be as close as I'll get to her again.

Our group has changed in the last couple of years of playing together. In the beginning there was so much toxicity on the courts. If you were playing at the wrong level and hurting another player's chance for improvement, you were considered anathema. Get lost. Go find players at your own level. How many times did people walk away when they saw me on the court? How much backbiting did I hear from players about each other? We constantly judged each other. In a subtle way—and sometimes not so kindly—we hounded people out of the group if they could barely serve or return a ball. We were not always nice, I'm sorry to admit.

Now, several years later, we've jelled into a friendly bunch of picklers. I detect a less judgmental attitude among us and more concern for one another. We share good news and bad; we discuss our personal challenges at length. I know more intimate details about some of the players than I do about my three sons, who rarely confide in me; or about my grandchildren, who never feel the urge to tell me about their knees or lungs. In the pickleball group I'm always ready to hear about someone's mother-in-law who had a fall in her seniors' residence, or a daughter who bought a new house before selling her current one. My pickleball partners and opponents are no longer just players who revert to being strangers when the game is over. They're a network of responsive individuals, a circle of care for anyone in need of help, like Sylvia.

As soon as the High Holy Days are over, I decide to set up a new chat group on WhatsApp to share information about Sylvia's disappearance, although I'm worried that the WhatsApp site is not secure enough to post highly sensitive data. What if her husband or those goons Sylvia befriended discover our chat group and find a way to read our messages? Sure, the WhatsApp folks say that messages and calls are end-to-end encrypted, but I don't trust the internet any further than I can throw a dime. Cyberattacks happen frequently on all sorts of sites. Even the Toronto Public Library is not immune to a ransomware attack. What is this world coming to? Life in the good old days was so much more honourable. (Anyone who believes that is lying.)

For all the above reasons, I hesitate to put Sylvia's name in the title of our WhatsApp group. Be positive, I tell myself. And outsmart them. I weigh my words as I mull over the first message to be posted on our new WhatsApp site, disarmingly called In 2 Win. Staring at my iPhone on my kitchen counter, I'm tense as I describe what I know about Sylvia's situation, which admittedly isn't much, but enough, I suspect, to provoke fears for Sylvia's life. Terrifying as it is, we can't dismiss the possibility that we'll never see Sylvia again.

[Heidi Allen created this group]

Dear pickleball friends. I invite you to join the In 2 Win chat for those of us in the pickleball community who know Sylvia Greene and would like to play with her again. If you haven't already heard, Sylvia's been absent from pickleball for many weeks. She didn't communicate with any of us about her plans to be away. Her husband hasn't provided any information on her whereabouts. She simply vanished. I'll release whatever daily information I've collected about Sylvia's situation. Please feel free to post any intelligence you may have on Sylvia's disappearance.

A torrent of messages follows:

[Liz] May the coming year bring u joyous pickleball games and no injuries. Top of my list: find Sylvia. We're In 2 Win this one. Shana tova

[Sharon] Most of all, find Sylvia and good health to you and your families

[Rebecca] A sweet new year to all my pickleball peeps. May we have Sylvia playing with us again soon. Anyone have new strategies to find her? I'm In 2 Win

[Marilyn] Where does Sylvia live? Should we take turns staking out her house?

[Lisa] Thumbs up

[Claudia] Dear picklers. I wish you all the best for a good sweet year and ask for forgiveness for any harm I have caused you throughout this year of pickleball. I'm available to stake out Sylvia's house on certain days of the week

[Laurie] I've got New Year's leftover honey cake. Anyone want some? It's delicious. I'd love to take a piece to Sylvia

[Heidi] Her address is 57 Shoremount. Not far from the courts on Maple Drive

[Ron] I grew up two blocks from there. My family loved to go out to eat at Pancer's nearby on Bathurst

[Heidi] Do you know anyone still living around there?

[Ron] Not anymore. Sorry

The idea of a stakeout intrigues me. Mr. Google says we need to have a car with tinted windows so we're unnoticeable. It's best to cover the licence plate of our stakeout car to remain anonymous. If we park directly across the street from Sylvia's house, we won't be able to see anything because the front foliage is so damn thick. But if we park across the street and several houses to the north, we'll be able to see across her driveway and have a view of the front door as well, which will allow us to spot anyone entering or leaving the house, like Sylvia. If we could just see Sylvia to make sure she's alright, that would be a big relief. We'd also pick up any suspicious activity going on in the house. Is her husband involved with another woman? Maybe he kicked Sylvia out, but she's too embarrassed to tell us. Where is she?

We may need blankets in the stakeout car because it's already getting chilly at night.

After I review the WhatsApp posts four times, I realize that we are pickleball friends, not ace detectives-in-waiting. Before we get too swept away, I post the following:

> [Heidi] If we don't find Sylvia soon, I'm planning to file a missing person's report with the police re: Sylvia's disappearance and see what happens

> [Ron] Good idea, Heidi Don't worry. U've got an army of picklers behind you. We won't let you down. BTW, Sylvia might be away on vacation in the south of France or Portugal, very popular tourist destination now. Did you check out that possibility? Another place to check is local hospitals and rehab facilities. She could have fallen and is in recovery somewhere. Things will work out. They always do. In 2 Win

> [Heidi] U cld be right, but if Sylvia is in a hospital or on vacation she'd text one of us. We're her friends

I turn off my phone and look in the fridge for a snack to distract me. An apple or grapefruit won't do the trick. My gut tells me there's something up with Sylvia, and I'm not prepared to minimize it. I'm tired of being told not to worry, tired of being assured that everything will work out, tired of playing guessing games. It's time to lean on her sordid husband Danny Greene for the facts. Without his involvement in our search for Sylvia, the odds of finding Sylvia are next to nil.

CHAPTER 23

Irene

September 2023

Dear Lord Almighty. Where has loving care gone to? Mamaleh is getting weaker by the minute, and Heidi is not visiting her as often as she should. She's always out playing that pickle game. She must be the pickle queen by now, but she also seems more anxious than usual. Getting her mother to read from her tablet was a bad idea, if you ask me. Why would a daughter encourage her ninety-three-year-old mother to remember all the horrible events in her life? It's like pushing her mommy into the grave. Heidi can't deal with her mother's story anyway. It's too hard for her. I feel so sad for these two women. One lost a mother and the other lost a grandmother in such a violent way. It's terrible, terrible. There's a saying my father often repeated to us kids back in the Philippines: "Without a mother, the home is broken." That's what happened to Mamaleh when her mommy died in the attic. Their home broke apart. The child was motherless.

I understand because I feel guilty myself for leaving my son, Winston, behind when I decided to take a job as a healthcare worker in Canada. I broke our home apart. But what choice did I have? I was a single parent, working full time at a private hospital and part time as a clinical instructor in Manila before I came to Canada. I used to daydream about bringing my son here. I imagined myself standing at the window watching him jump in big snow drifts and building a snowman with raisins for eyes and a carrot nose. We'd have a white Christmas. That would never happen in the Philippines because it doesn't snow there. But those dreams were from many years ago. My son was still a small child then.

I decided to leave my family, church, and two jobs behind to work abroad to earn more money for him and my parents. That way I can send him to university someday. I know that he cries when he does not see me every day, but I can't afford to bring him here. I don't earn enough to raise him and also save for his education.

One day last winter I did not have enough money for the subway fare back to my apartment. I was working as a personal support worker in Etobicoke, and I was one dollar short of the fare until my salary cheque arrived in my bank account the next day. That was my low point, the most discouraging day of my life. I threw myself at the mercy of a TTC employee, who said, "Go back to the Philippines or tell your sob story to a psychiatrist." Lucky for me, he let me get on the subway, and I made it back to my apartment. But my story is not unusual. Dear Lord, I pray that you will please help the thousands of women like me who leave the Philippines each year for better career opportunities in Canada. Sometimes these better opportunities don't turn out the way we dreamed, or it takes a lot longer than we imagined to reach our goals. My son and I have been separated too long. I'm also separated from my mommy and daddy who are getting old, and I'm not there to take care of them. When Covid happened, I was working in a long-term facility in Canada. Many workers were getting Covid. Some died. I had to leave the long-term care facility to preserve my health. I didn't want Winston to become an orphan. Lord, don't let that happen.

Mamaleh moans and calls for me. She is getting weaker and weaker. Today I can hardly hear her voice. I stay by her side, reading books to her, or we watch television together until she drifts off to sleep. When she awakes, I slice the green grapes in half for her if Heidi remembers to bring Mamaleh a bunch. It's unkind when Heidi forgets about her dying mommy.

CHAPTER 24

Mamaleh

Recording 07.mp4

1944. I returned to the closet in the attic after my mother died, sure about one thing: I would never leave this space again, not even to pee. I sat scrunched into a ball, my arms coiled around my knees, exactly where I was when I touched her body for the last time. Mendl tried to coax me to come out. He brought a hunk of bread and soup broth upstairs, but I pushed away the food. In the closet I floated into a dream in which I was caught in a storm on a rough sea. My grandmother Ruth rescued me. She placed my head in her lap and stroked my eyebrows with her fingertips. I prayed that Grandma would never know that her own daughter was murdered in her attic.

After a few days passed, my father lifted me out of the closet. Scooping my near-lifeless body in his arms, he carried me downstairs to the bedroom. I spent most days staring out the window, gazing at the oak trees lining the end of the garden, pretending that Mother was still alive. She'd always be alive for me. Once the funeral and the formal seven-day period of mourning concluded, I overheard Father tell Mendl that it was unsafe for a young girl like me to remain in Szczniki. Anti-Jewish violence was on the rise. Pogroms were cropping up across Poland. He heard of teenage Jewish girls being raped and abandoned. My purity, he insisted, must always be protected.

Within a fortnight Father arranged for my departure from Szczniki, while Mendl would stay behind to resurrect the family tannery business alongside him. Early on my last morning at home, before anyone else in the household stirred, just before my unwanted separation from the only people and place I knew and loved, I tiptoed up the stairs to the attic. I had to see the closet again. I crawled inside and put my lips on the spot where I hugged Mother before we separated from each other.

The few possessions I carried on my journey were a couple of studio photos that Father managed to retrieve from Challah's sandbox where he had hastily stashed them on the night of our escape from Szczniki. My favourite snapshot of me feeding the chickens one summer day in the country, I hid in my shoe. I pulled hard on the shoelaces and tied a double knot to make sure the picture stayed hidden there. I tucked the studio photos into my underwear, strapping the envelope in place with a thick leather belt.

I travelled westward as the daughter of my father's friends, Mr. and Mrs. Lau, who had survived imprisonment in Auschwitz. Father believed I would be safer as a member of their family than being on my own. We crossed one border after another, and each time we concealed my identity from the officials who subjected all of my travel documents to careful inspection. We went from Poland to Czechoslovakia, bound for a displaced persons camp in northern Germany.

At each checkpoint along the route, I looked the border guard directly in the eye and declared that I was Roza Lau, the child of Menachem and Rena Lau. If anyone discovered that my identity documents were forged, I feared that I would be declared stateless and ineligible for refugee status.

Whenever I missed my family, I pressed down on the snapshot stashed in my shoe or patted my belly to feel the larger photos strapped around my waist. I only removed the pictures when I slept or sponge-bathed. Each time I stared at the pictures, I noticed a new crease or a curling corner. I wondered if I would be able to hold on to those photos forever. Would the images always be visible or would my old life fade away?

CHAPTER 25

Heidi

September 2023

I'm at Mamaleh's side as she reads from her tablet. Her voice is not as vigorous as it used to be, but she's still present. I can't imagine Maple Drive without her. Her universe was demolished, and yet she managed to reinvent herself under new circumstances. Irene props Mamaleh's bony body against the pillows to ensure her comfort. When I bend over to kiss her forehead, I see Mamaleh's pink scalp beneath the pixie haircut Irene keeps impeccably cropped. Mamaleh nods and gives me a wan smile.

"Where's that photo you hid in your shoe?" I ask.

"What?"

"The photo, the one you put in your shoe? When you left Poland. Remember?"

"Shoe? Where are my shoes?"

"No, Mamaleh. The picture you put in your shoe. What happened to it?"

She closes her eyes rather than responding. Soon she'll be asleep. I turn to Irene to ask about her son.

"How old is Winston now?"

"He's a teenager. He's going to high school soon and then to university, I hope."

"In the Philippines?" I ask.

"I can't afford to bring him here."

Mamaleh's eyes spring open. "Bring him here, Irene. I'll pay and you can both live here."

Really! Where did that crazed notion come from? Mamaleh never offered to bring Irene's son to Canada before. Or have them live in this house! True, she's always been philanthropic and still is. Her name often appears on the donor list of foundations, such as the Hospital for Sick Children and the Art Gallery of Ontario. She and Dad invested wisely in Toronto real estate over the years so that Mamaleh was financially secure when he died. I know next to nothing about my father's early life, but I do know that he was a good provider. Thanks to him and the estate of my deceased husband, Bernie, I don't need Mamaleh's money. Nor do my two oldest sons, who are both lawyers. It's my youngest son, Simon, a public school teacher, that I worry about. Teachers can hardly afford to own a house in Toronto these days without help.

To be sure, Mamaleh's offer to bring Irene's son, Winston, to Canada is generous, but it's also unrealistic. Where would they live in Toronto in the long term? Rents are skyrocketing. How would Irene be able to support Winston in Canada and still send money back to her parents in the Philippines? Okay, I understand that Mamaleh wants Irene and her son to have a nice home to live in. Irene has taken great care of Mamaleh and this house. She has scrubbed every inch of it. Mamaleh appreciates that. But to me, the whole idea of Irene and her son living here is out of the question because I've always assumed that Simon would inherit Mamaleh's house on Maple Drive.

The house of my childhood must stay in this family. I want my grandchildren Chloe and Tyler to live across from the park where I played as a kid and still do play. I once asked Mamaleh how we ended up on Maple Drive, and she said she loved the apple trees in the park. I have fond memories of those trees too. The older I get, the more I crave continuity with my formative years. I may be on the decline physically—I'm at the age when looking in the mirror is scarier than a horror movie. Who is that ancient woman with the coarse wrinkles and saggy skin staring back at me? Still, I'm keen to preserve the vitality of my younger self for as long as I can. Simon and his family living on Maple Drive will be a constant reminder of who I was and who I want to remain.

Before taking off for the pickleball courts, I kiss Mamaleh's forehead again and pat her veiny hand. I'll make sure that Irene receives a big bonus when Mamaleh leaves this earth. Of course I will, because that's what she would want. I'll honour the intent of her wishes, more or less.

Make that less. I'm not as charitable as she is.

Questions and comments about Sylvia monopolize the bench talk as soon as I arrive at the courts. Everyone agrees to ditch the stakeout plan because it's unrealistic. Not a single pickler owns a vehicle with tinted windows, nor does anyone relish spending the night holed up in a car waiting for action at 57 Shoremount to happen.

"Hey, guys," Ron cuts in. "Let's play. I hate to be a spoilsport, but I don't have all day. Some of us have jobs, you know. Heidi, Liz, Lisa, are you good to go?"

"Sure thing," Liz says.

"Me too," I add, but that's a lie. Intrusive thoughts about Mamaleh, Irene, and Sylvia distract me from engaging in the match.

"Okay, Heidi. Serve already," Liz shouts from across the court. "What are you waiting for, Godot or something?"

I'm in no mood to play, and worse still, I'll wreck the game for the others. Samantha, a beginner who has already surpassed my level of play—fucking hell, how did that happen?—offers to take my place. I shrug and slip off the court, too embarrassed to say goodbye. Instead of shopping for Mamaleh on my way home, I drive directly to my condo and park, fearful as I exit my car in the dimly lit underground garage.

On the elevator ride up to my unit, I anticipate what sort of information I'll need to file a missing person report on Sylvia. Shutting my eyes, I conjure up the last time I saw her. I picture Sylvia leaving Maple Drive Park with that creep Joe. I remember watching her walk too close to him as he limped along. I was confused when they turned left toward Bathurst Street rather than right toward her house on Shoremount. I should have chased after her then, tried to stop her, called out her name, but I didn't.

She wasn't herself that day. That's what stands out for me the most. She wasn't the Sylvia I know. She had yanked her baseball cap ludicrously far down on her forehead to hide the swelling of her face. Her cat-eye sunglasses were so large that she constantly had to adjust them to prevent the silly things from landing on the tip of her nose. Even her oversized grey sweatshirt with deep pockets differed from her usual slim-fitting hoodie. Why was Sylvia dressed as someone else?

Walking from the elevator to my condo, I search inside my purse for the keys, but I can't find them. I dig around in my pickleball bag, but no, I didn't toss them in there. I retrace my steps to the underground garage, thinking I might have left them on the front seat of the car. Maybe, by some miracle, I'll find Sylvia waiting in the passenger's seat, smiling as if nothing happened. I told you not to worry about me, she'll say. The condo keys are there, but not Sylvia. That's the moment I know she's gone.

It's dusk by the time I contact the police about Sylvia's disappearance, and there's little to no ambient light in my living room. I switch on a lamp to input the phone number for filing a missing person report. I've checked the Pickleball Organizer. The last time I saw Sylvia was Thursday, August 17, 2023.

The attending officer who answers my call speaks with a Jamaican accent, her voice as reassuring as a pilot's during periods of turbulence. She asks me for a physical description of Sylvia, which I provide without difficulty. But when the officer requests the names of her family members as well as information on her physical and mental health, I falter.

"Ms. Allen, are you still there?"

"Her husband's name is Danny Greene," I say. "I wish I could be of more help, but the truth is, Sylvia Greene did not behave like the Sylvia Greene I know on the day she went missing. She walked off the court with a man she barely knew, turned the wrong way, and vanished. I'm sorry. That's as much as I know."

"I see. Can you provide a photo of Sylvia Greene? It will greatly assist in our investigation. We can use it in a news release and social media posts to draw attention to the case, which may prompt useful leads. Of course, we'll contact her husband first."

"A photo? I don't have one, though it's possible that others in our pickleball network do. I'm so sorry that I can't be more helpful. I do have her home address and cell phone number. Would you like me to give you the information?"

"Yes please. A police officer will contact you for additional data, including the names of significant people in Sylvia's life, such as family and friends, their phone numbers and email addresses, as well Sylvia's banking and credit card information, her driver's licence, and passport."

"I'm afraid I don't have access to any of that. Maybe her husband can assist you. He lives at 57 Shoremount."

"I see. Perhaps you can answer this: Where does Sylvia go most often? Does she have favourite places where we might expect to find her?"

"On a pickleball court. She usually plays with us on Maple Drive."

How superficial my response must sound. I doubt that anyone would surmise I'm even moderately attached to Sylvia from the sparse information I provided. But I am. Even if I've only known her for a relatively short time, we just clicked. There are people I need to carry with me, like long-lost family. Sylvia's one of them. But hey, friends are the family we choose for ourselves. Until they're not.

"Thank you for contacting us," the attending police officer says. My living room is dark when I hang up, except for a sliver of moonlight illuminating the windowsill.

CHAPTER 26

Sylvia

September 2023

At least I'm locked in my own study. There's some comfort in that. I've always liked the fact that my home office is at the front of the house. I can see the cars travelling along Shoremount, often exceeding the speed limit. With so many young families living in this neighbourhood again, that's frightening. Only a few of the older, original owners are still here. Most of the seniors have moved into condos farther north. We should have done that too. Owning a condo would mean less maintenance, increased security, and lock-and-leave travel possibilities instead of being isolated in this big deteriorating house that we can't maintain anymore.

All those lost opportunities to ponder while I'm incarcerated in this room. *Should have, could have*—I repeat these phrases far too many times per day. In the meantime, here I sit, clogging my lungs with the stale air in my study. I can't open the window to get a fresh breeze because my dear husband has made that impossible. Does he think I'll jump from the second floor, or that a kidnapper will climb up and liberate me? Yeah, right. When pigs fly. What's bothering me the most are the dirty white curtains hanging in this room. I could ask Danny to wash them, but I doubt he would be amenable to that. He isn't even washing my clothes. I've been wearing the same underwear for weeks now. And sleeping on the pull-out sofa bed in my study isn't helping my back much either. In the morning when I get up, I can't stand up straight.

At first, life without the internet was a refreshing experience, but now I feel completely cut off. I don't have a clue about what's happening in the outside world. I do have books in my study to keep me company, but most of them are math textbooks I used decades before, when I was going to become a mathematician. I haven't touched them since grad school. What's the point? All hopes of ever becoming a math prof died long ago. There are a few novels still on the shelves, although most of the fiction went to Goodwill. Let others have the pleasure of losing themselves in a good story.

I force myself to investigate the bookshelves. The palm of my hand presses into my sore lower back while I skim the titles in my shrunken fiction collection. The mysteries don't interest me. Louise Penny, John Grisham. No thank you. My fingers walk along the spines of books until I find a novel that suits my mood. It's lying crosswise on the shelf, wedged into the gap between the top of the upright books and the shelving above. Old and battered, and the book jacket is a little torn, but the title and author are still legible.

Anna Karenina by Leo Tolstoy.

I pull the book out, blow the dust off the cover, and open it with caution to avoid ripping the brittle pages. Turning to the first chapter, I read aloud the opening line. "All happy families are alike; each unhappy family is unhappy in its own way."

I sigh and shrug. I always expected the unhappiness in our little family to dissolve over time, but our unhappy bits were not minor occurrences in an otherwise harmonious marriage. Danny's jealousy and his obsession with punishing me have never changed. I remember once staying at the office after hours to attend a retirement party for the kindest accountant, a gentle man whom I worked with for years. By the time I left the gathering, it was rush hour, and the subway was packed. I missed several trains before I was able to get on and didn't arrive home until seven o'clock. Danny was furious that he had no dinner. He accused me of sneaking out for a date with one of the accountants. That absurd accusation ended with a shiner. The next day he refused to let me go to work with a black eye. I had to call in sick. Because of my absence, the office was short-staffed. I hated leaving my colleagues in the lurch like that. It was unlike me. I pride myself on being reliable, predictable Sylvia. So the second morning I put on sunglasses and returned to work, explaining to anyone who asked that the dark glasses alleviated the symptoms of my conjunctivitis. If nothing else, I am an accomplished liar.

Maybe I'm being too hard on good old Danny boy. I could be wrong about him. It's possible that I'm responsible for our unhappy family.

This morning there wasn't enough food on the tray he brought me, and my hungry stomach has been talking to me ever since. Three days ago he stood at the door and watched me as I devoured a bowl of cereal, slurping the last drop of milk and begging with my eyes for more. He crossed the room to collect the bowl and put his arms around me. "You know I love you," he said. "I'll always take care of you."

I pushed him away. "Is this how you take care of someone you love?"

"Don't be angry with me," he said. "Let's make up."

"Make up for what?"

"Sylvia, you're not only involved in drug dealing, I think you've been cheating on me too. You're a whore. I've seen the messages on your phone from some guy who keeps texting you. I also found money in your purse. More than I'd pay. He must really enjoy you."

"Stop, Danny." I backed away from him.

"No," he snarled. "You can't do this to me and get away with it."

When I awoke the next morning, I was curled up on the carpet, naked. I felt blood caked on my face, and my inner thighs were bruised. I couldn't lift my head.

CHAPTER 27

Mamaleh

Recording 08.mp4

1948–1949. I was one of the youngest patients in the hospital ward reserved for tubercular patients. Hardly a medal-worthy achievement. The nurses and doctors took an immediate liking to me because I was an easy patient compared with the seven hundred typhus victims that needed to be bathed and rubbed with anti-lice powder almost every day. Next to them, I was as uncomplicated as an inert log. On the wall at the foot of my bed, head nurse Ursula taped a large sheet of paper with the rules for TB patients inked in thick black letters:

1. No baths
2. No movement except to toilet twice a day
3. No sitting up except propped by pillows and semi-reclining
4. No sewing, knitting, or writing, except as occasional relief from reading and sleeping

Impossible. If I followed her orders, I'd have soon been a big fat turnip. I decided I had to put those exceptions to good use and get the hospital staff to help me out.

When the kind nurse Gretchen was not too frazzled, I asked her to sit me up very straight. She agreed and even let me wear her little white cap while she took my temperature. I felt taller and healthier already. And there was a handsome young German intern completing his *Praktisches Jahr* named Herman—Herman Petersen, his badge said—who was passionate about football, cycling, tennis, sprinting— any sport that favours being fit and making friends. He loved telling me stories about one of Germany's most famous tennis players, Gottfried von Cramm. Herman idolized him. It turned out that von Cramm had an affair with a Jew during the Nazi era. How courageous was that!

Herman was also brave. He challenged head nurse Ursula's rules by telling me that I didn't have to restrict my movement so severely. I could do light exercises, starting with deep breathing. "Well, not too deep," he said, then laughed, and I laughed too. According to him, I could be out of here in six months. But honestly, I was more worried about my future than the time spent at the DP camp. I wondered if I would be able to have babies. Herman Petersen said, "Yes, why not?"

One day, several months after my admission to the hospital, Mr. and Mrs. Lau paid me a visit. They appeared at the door of the ward, looking relieved that at least I wasn't dead. It was so long since I last saw them that I almost didn't recognize them. They had promised my father they would take care of me. Yet both of them missed the symptoms of tuberculosis that nearly destroyed my lungs. They heard me coughing while I dressed for school. But they didn't want to take me to the hospital for fear that an administrator would discover the truth: Roza Lau was nothing but an imposter, a fake refugee, and a sad girl.

Mrs. Lau offered me a chocolate bar to cheer me up. She tried hard to make me smile by telling me tales from her childhood back home. I wasn't listening. I didn't bother to answer when she asked me how I felt. As far as I was concerned, the sooner they left, the better. Outside the door to the ward, I heard Mrs. Lau talking to the hospital staff.

"Take care of Roza," she said. "I beg you. You must keep her alive."

"She'll be fine." I recognized Herman's voice.

"You seem like a nice young man. You won't let anything happen to her, will you?"

When I was finally released from the hospital, I was eager to resume a normal life, if living in a DP camp could be called normal. I decided to join a group of young people from the camp who were going to visit a farming collective for the weekend. It sounded healthy and interesting to me, but Mr. and Mrs. Lau were against the trip because they were afraid that I would have a relapse. After I promised not to die, they insisted that a chaperone must go with me. That was silly, I told them. I was eighteen years old—an adult. I insisted that neither one of them was allowed to come with me. Mrs. Lau tapped her toe on the floor.

"We'll see about that," she said.

On a Friday afternoon, just before the truck departed, I climbed aboard and squeezed between two people already seated. I looked around for a familiar face, and saw only one: Herman Petersen.

"What are you doing here?" I said.

"I'm heading home, done with my internship," Herman said. "When Mrs. Lau came to the hospital to ask if I could go with you to the training farm, I agreed. It's on my way home anyway."

"So you're the chaperone."

"You could say that."

The road was brimming with buses, horse-drawn wagons, bicycles, and people on foot. Everyone in Europe seemed to be on the move, searching for somebody or something. I was searching for somebody or something too. Thanks to Mrs. Lau, Herman watched over me like a hawk-eyed bodyguard on high alert. But he was not always so serious. On Saturday afternoon, when we were walking through the apple orchard on the farm, Herman picked up a smooth-skinned yellow apple from the ground and gave it to me.

"Very tart." I tossed it away. "When I get out of the DP camp and leave Germany, I want to have a big garden with cherry trees so I can soak the cherries in brandy and make drunken cherries, like my parents did in Poland."

"Me too. I want a whole apple orchard and pear trees and..." Herman started spinning around and around with his arms outstretched, palms tilted upward, and his face smiling up at the sky. I did the same little dance until we both fell to the ground.

However, on Sunday, during my last meal of the weekend and after Herman had left on his journey home, I took a bite of a sweet, tasty bun. When I bit down, I got a terrible toothache. Not that I was surprised. During the war, toothbrushes, like wristwatches, went missing and were never found. Nobody had toothbrushes in the cave where we hid, nor was anybody worried about the state of their teeth. We were too preoccupied with daily survival.

Though I sponged my face with warm water and gargled as soon as I returned to the DP camp, my tooth continued to hurt. I had no choice but to visit the dental clinic, where I was lucky to meet Haskel Alinsky, a young dental technician wearing a white lab coat over his street clothes. "I'm sorry," he said after he examined the bleeding and swelling around my sore tooth. "The tooth can't be saved. Extraction is required, and then a false tooth will be necessary."

From the moment I met Hal, I trusted him. He grew up in a shtetl like I did. While pulling out my tooth, he told me that his father had been a kosher butcher. In 1940 a friend of Hal's was going to Budapest to become a dental technician. Hal decided to follow him. He said it was the best decision he ever made. Leaving Poland saved him. And, as luck would have it, Hal saved me from a miserable future too.

About a year or so later, Mrs. Lau made a wedding for Hal and me at the DP camp. Nothing extravagant. Just a few jars of herring and a honey cake bought on the black market. Like everyone else in the DP camp, we wanted to start a new family as quickly as possible. It seemed that every other woman was either pregnant or pushing a baby carriage at the Bergen-Belsen DP camp. Soon I became one of them.

CHAPTER 28

Heidi

October 2023

Irene and I help Mamaleh into bed after she finishes reading from her tablet. "Let me get this straight," I say to my mother. "If you had brushed your teeth regularly during the war and hadn't gotten a toothache, I might not exist. I owe my birth to a bloody decaying tooth in your mouth, which resulted in you meeting the dental technician who became my father, right?"

She nods. "Something like that." On her night table sits the familiar green plastic container for her dentures.

When Irene brings us tea, I smell a fruity, medicinal scent coming from her cup. "Do you have a toothache?" I observe Irene pressing her fingers to her jaw.

"Just a little pain," she whimpers.

"You need to go to the dentist. Too bad my father's no longer alive to help you. He could fix your tooth in a jiffy," I say, with a pang of sorrow over his absence. "His patients often gave him little gifts to show their appreciation. He never missed a day of work or refused to help someone in an emergency."

"A dentist? No, no. Not necessary." After a pause Irene admits the truth. "Dentists cost too much anyway."

"But you might need an antibiotic." Looking more closely at her, I detect a bit of swelling near the jawline.

"The pain will go away soon," she says. She bends over to feel Mamaleh's cheeks, flushed from the hot tea. "Boiled guava leaves are a good cure for infections."

I stand up, arms entwined behind my back, watching Irene coddle my mother, encouraging her to close her eyes and take a nap. For a moment, I'm jealous of the tight connection between Irene and Mamaleh. They seem more like a family than a caregiver and a patient. I want to interrupt and say, "Hey, guys. What about me?"

I'm flooded with envy until I hear a ping on the WhatsApp chat. My pickleball network beckons:

[Liz] Hey Heidi. R u playing this aft? Any news on the missing person's file? Have the police found Sylvia?

[Heidi] Nothing to report. Sorry

[Liz] What's taking so long? She could be dead by the time they find her

[Heidi] Don't even go there

[Lisa] Maybe we should hire a private detective

[Heidi] Got somebody in mind?

[Lisa] Nope. Haven't needed one so far

[Liz] See u courtside soon. BTW here's a recipe for chocolate chip gluten-free cookies

[Heidi] Thank u, looks yummy. I'm so worried I'll probably eat them all

I'm late to my 2:30 p.m. game. Lacing up my court shoes, I notice a new woman playing with our group. She's taller, younger, and better than anyone else. I wonder if she was a tennis prodigy in a previous life or maybe she started playing squash when she was in diapers. Her flawless appearance makes me feel like a shrivelled septuagenarian. Suddenly the fence gate clangs open. A skinny, scruffy figure lopes toward us wearing jeans so low on his butt that his pants could easily slide down to his knees. It takes me a moment to realize that he's Joe, that creepy guy who might have kidnapped Sylvia.

"Where is she?" he barks at me. No hello. No sign of concern for Sylvia's well-being. Just plain rudeness, which makes me wonder how sweet, polite Sylvia ever got mixed up with this sicko.

"I have no idea where Sylvia is. I thought you'd be the one to know." The only response I get is a growl, like a raccoon trying to terrorize a squirrel. What's next, I wonder—biting and clawing?

"Where does she live?" he snaps after a few moments.

"How should I know." I'm beginning to feel threatened by the hostility in his voice.

"You're lying." When he takes several steps toward me, I step back. He stinks, like a stray cat pissed on his jeans. I start to shiver, though the air is warm enough to spoil the tuna-and-egg sandwich in my bag.

"Someone call the police!" I yell, but he takes off before any of us has a chance to phone 911. I sit down on the bench and stare into space, worried what he'll do to Sylvia if he finds her before we do.

CHAPTER 29

Jonathan

October 2023

Why the fuck did Heidi add me to this pickleball WhatsApp chat thing? The posts of these women are often hysterical. Oops. Sexist language. Scratch it. The messages are frantic, overwrought, and seriously agitated. I'm getting pings about every five minutes on my phone, but I can't stop reading every one of them. I need to have the latest info on Sylvia. When Heidi titled this chat group In 2 Win, she got that right. We absolutely must find her. But if Sylvia's in so much shit, why the hell didn't she contact me? Whatever she wants or needs, I'll do it. No need for the police to become involved. Jesus H. Christ. More pings.

> [Heidi] Hey pickleball friends. Today the scariest thing happened on the Maple Drive courts. A strange man named Joe showed up. Sylvia met him here this summer and became friends with him. He smells like cat piss and was looking for Sylvia. Trust me, if he returns, stay away from him. Don't give him any info. He says he doesn't know where she lives or where she is now. Don't engage with him at all.

The last time I saw Sylvia, she was leaving the courts with him. He knows much more than he's telling us

[Ron] Joe who?

[Heidi] Don't know

[Joanne] Maybe he's a drug dealer or a pervert

[Liz] Here's a video I took while Heidi was talking to him today. Creepy

[Lisa] Send it to police

[Liz] What should I say?

[Lisa] Don't know. Don't have playbook for this kind of thing. Does anyone?

[Jonathan] What can I do to help?

[Ron] What an unholy mess Sylvia has gotten herself into

[Lisa] Why did she go off with this thug in first place? Why would she do something so strange?

[Joanne] Must be reason for her to behave so impulsively, totally out of character

[Heidi] Or was she taking calculated risk? Sometimes taking big risk is better than doing nothing. Doing nothing is also running risk. Right?

[Lisa] You've been reading too many mysteries

[Heidi] Bullshit. I noticed something strange in her behaviour well before all of this happened. Nothing major, but maybe she was mixed up in something before this summer

[Liz] Why were those hoodlums on Maple Drive that night anyway? They're not from around here. Smells fishy to me

[Ron] Because they could be in the park and drink at the same time thanks to the new City of Toronto pilot project. Remember.

[Lisa] OMG. Always knew it was bad idea. Alcohol in the park. Can only lead to problems

[Jonathan] That's yr opinion. Very few people complained about drinking in parks. I haven't seen any incidents reported in the media so there you go.

[Heidi] It only takes one incident so there you go right back.

[Jonathan] These posts are getting testy. Anyone want to play pickleball with me to de-escalate? I can offer an afternoon of free pickleball coaching. Let's play and have fun. Sylvia, wherever she is, would want that

[Heidi] When?

[Jonathan] I'm available this weekend. How about Saturday 3 p.m. Maple Drive courts. All welcome, weather permitting. Sign up on the Pickleball Organizer, 6 people to a court. Let's try to get all three courts going at the same time. I'll rotate and coach. Deal?

Instead of eighteen people showing up on Saturday, about thirty-five people crowd the three courts. That's seventeen more players than I can handle. They range in age from thirty-five to eighty-five. Slightly more women than men. It's a diverse group with one thing in common: an obsession with pickleball. They're serious enough to own expensive paddles and wear proper court shoes. But when I suggest that players divide into different courts based on their level of play—beginner, intermediate, and advanced—I get blowback. Not that I haven't dealt with this kind of stuff a hundred times before. It's always the same. Everybody thinks they're advanced. Nobody wants to be a beginner. Yet beginner and advanced players will steal intermediate spots to get a game.

"Hey, folks," I shout. "Come over here for a minute. Let's not waste time arguing about who belongs on which court."

I hear some grumbling. A few players leave. Those remaining sort themselves into various teams. Easy peasy, I'm thinking, when two police officers stride onto the court.

"Hey, what's going on?" I ask Heidi.

Heidi looks as stunned as I am. "Who called the police? What in the hell are they doing here?"

"Good afternoon," one officer says. "Do any of you know Sylvia Greene?"

"How did they know we'd be here now?" I ask Heidi.

"Looks like our WhatsApp account was hacked. Just what I thought might happen. A lot of good my innocuous title did us."

"If anyone knows Sylvia Greene or has any information about her whereabouts, please contact us. We'd like to hear from you. Anything you know would be helpful." The police officers watch our faces, waiting for some sort of reveal from one of us. After a few minutes of silence, they pass around their cards. "Thank you for your time. Enjoy your game."

Hold on, I'm tempted to say. What about an update on Sylvia's disappearance? A little show of urgency wouldn't hurt either. But what did I expect? The truth is, police investigations into disappearances can be seriously flawed. I've heard from clients about searches that are disorganized, incomplete, or inadequately documented. And I wouldn't be surprised if the police don't make the disappearance of seniors a high priority anyway. Inadequate resources. Expectations that the safety and well-being of old people are the domain of social services, public health, and community agencies. Outdated reporting procedures. You name it. A quiet sixty-something woman like Sylvia could slip through the cracks.

I just want to know where you are, Sylvia. It's hard to be in this world without you.

CHAPTER 30

Sylvia

October 2023

I'm not sure how long I can go on like this. But I can't give up either. I know that. I can't just sit locked up in this room, drowning in a puddle of self-pity. Thankfully, something steely inside me forces my muscles to work, pushes me to keep exercising my quads and my biceps every day. I do at least twenty circles around this room for cardio in the morning and at night, holding a heavy book in each hand. But the other part of my mind says just give up and give in. Make up with the bastard. Do what he wants you to do. Never go to the courts on Maple Drive, never see Heidi, Jonathan, or the rest of the pickleball group again. Be a solitary prisoner forever in this miserable house. No, it would be impossible to do that. I refuse to capitulate to Danny's demands, at least not now. And I won't stop playing pickleball no matter what he says. He can call me a stupid shit as much as he wants. When he says, "If I can't have you, no one else can either," I will train myself not to listen.

Looking out the window, I don't see another soul walking on Shoremount. I notice several cop cars driving up and down our block, slowing in front of our house. I wonder if someone called the police. I don't know, but I doubt it. No officers have come to our door.

Unfortunately, I don't think cops in a car would hear me banging against the window of my study, because the house is set so far back from the street. I could shatter the window and jump, but it's a long way down. I've always had an intense fear of heights, even as a child. We lived in one of those two-storey Tudors with a dark stairwell and an uncarpeted staircase. Every day I worried about mounting those stairs and breaking my neck on the way down. I never go out on the balcony when visiting my friends in high-rise condos downtown. I lie that it's too windy or too hot or too cramped. Whatever. Once when Danny and I were at his cousin's condo in Thornhill, he insisted I have drinks on their small balcony with the family. I was trembling so much that I spilled red wine on my faded jeans. I immediately blotted the wine spot with a paper towel, though I didn't want to make a scene by asking the host for club soda or kosher salt to remove the stain completely. Danny would have hit the ceiling if I'd inconvenienced his cousin. By the time we came home, I was too exhausted to finish the tedious job. In all the times I've washed those jeans afterward, that stubborn stain has never gone away.

I wonder if that's an unmarked police car parked across the street. Maybe some sort of stakeout or surveillance is underway. Could be, but I don't really know. Best to keep quiet. Not to speak, not to tap on the window.

It's safest just to watch. That's all.

CHAPTER 31

Mamaleh

Recording 09.mp4

1950. I wanted to give birth at the Glyn-Hughes Hospital in the DP camp. I felt safe there. I survived tuberculosis in the hospital's TB ward. Thanks God. In that hospital I was given a second chance. I'll never forget the good care the nurses and the handsome intern gave me. The hospital's Department of Obstetrics and Gynecology, with one exhausted pediatrician, also had a strong reputation among the many refugee women who gave birth there.

Hinda Schreiber Alinsky was born on May 14, 1950. We named our daughter after my father, Haim, who died in a Russian gulag after the war. It was Mrs. Lau who affectionately nicknamed the baby Heidi because she always loved the children's story of Heidi, the orphan girl who found happiness in the Swiss Alps. We were skeptical at first, but the sound of the name brought music to our ears, like a *nigun*, one of those wordless Yiddish tunes sung over and over, like this: *Heidi, hei-di-de-Hei-di. Hei-di. Hei-di.*

And so it was. Hal, Heidi, and I settled into a single room on Block 89 in the DP camp, down the hall from Mr. and Mrs. Lau. Unwashed coffee cups often sat on the kitchen table when Hal went to work in the dental clinic each morning. His shirts hung on the backs of the only two chairs we had. The baby's crib occupied the middle of the room, not that it got much use. My little daughter hadn't figured out that people are supposed to sleep at night. I washed her diapers in the kitchen sink and dried them on the stove. Mrs. Lau visited shortly after breakfast every morning to help, and she was usually still there at noon. One morning she brought a tiny pink knitted cap made from yarn that Hal procured for her on the black market. Everyone knew that you could get just about anything on the black market for a price if you were smart. And Hal was very smart.

Looking at the baby playing with her feet, I'd bend over to stroke her smooth cheek. Nothing was more important to me than the feel of Heidi's skin and the sound of her gassy burps. Nothing. Not even the stories I tried to remember about Szczniki that sometimes I wrote down while Heidi was asleep, which was not so often.

When we finally received approval to come to Canada, we pleaded with Mr. and Mrs. Lau to come with us. We worried that the old couple might become ill with nobody to look after them. But they felt they were too set in their traditions to leave Europe. The five of us rode the bus from the DP camp to the German port of Bremerhaven on the North Sea, where the Alinsky family of three was scheduled to embark on our journey to Canada. When it was time to board the ship, I hugged Mrs. Lau for the first and last time. I never did warm up to this woman, who tried her best to care for me and asked for nothing in return.

Soon we joined the other passengers crowding together at the edge of the deck. We frantically threw kisses to Mr. and Mrs. Lau, who looked smaller and smaller as the ship pushed away from the shoreline. I waved Heidi's pudgy hand at them until she pulled it away from me.

Leaning against the ship's railing, I reviewed my experiences in Germany and the muddled feelings I had during the years I lived in the DP camp, caught in a kind of waiting room. Waiting for what? A future I couldn't imagine, a life without my birth family and my two hundred thirty-three relatives from Szczniki who perished. Though I didn't realize it then, there was also something beautiful about being at the DP camp. Yes, I was confused, always about to cry, but at the same time, I was trying to grab on to something new—searching, without knowing it, for what was possible after my whole world was snatched from me.

As the ship headed out to sea, the wind blew a strand of hair from my barrette. I wiggled my toes in the dark corner of my worn shoe, but the snapshot of me feeding the chickens was no longer there and hadn't been for a while. I watched Mr. and Mrs. Lau walk back to the bus for as long as my eyes held them in view. I knew they would never see me again, their adopted daughter who was and wasn't theirs.

"*Zeit gezunt*, Mr. and Mrs. Lau," I said. I turned away from the railing to find our cabin. *Auf Wiedersehen*, DP camp and the Glyn-Hughes Hospital where Heidi was born. We were ready to remake our lives. Instead of the Alinsky family, we would be the Allen family if we had the *mazel*—I meant the good luck—to reach Canada alive.

CHAPTER 32

Heidi

October 2023

Mamaleh concludes her reading and drops the tablet in her lap. There's nothing left for her to tell. She has finished conveying the story of her early life, sharing as much as I will ever need to know about her childhood and my birth. It's an unsettling moment for both of us, but not in the way I expected the end of her tablet would be. I've always assumed that whatever trauma she experienced as a child was passed along to me. Her fear of loss and her hypervigilance became mine. Careful, careful, careful—our core belief, our mantra. But that's not Mamaleh's whole story.

Listening to her read, I heard the voice of a woman who willed herself to start again. She witnessed the murder of her mother and endured the separation from her father, who dispatched her to a displaced persons camp in Germany, never to see him again. Yet somehow in the DP camp, that lonely space between her horrific past and her unknown future, she managed to give birth to a new self and a new baby, my life layered upon hers. As the episodes in her tablet unfolded, I watched her stumble, sometimes struggling to finish a sentence. But she kept going.

There's no doubt that I've inherited more than Mamaleh's wartime trauma and fearfulness. By example after example, she transmitted her tenacity to me. She demonstrated her inner game of survival that she kept playing until she won. This I know to be true: When Mamaleh fixates on something, she never lets it go. I only wish I had that concentration and a quiet mindset to compete under pressure in pickleball.

"Amen. You did it!" I put my arm around her shoulder and place her tablet on the coffee table in front of us.

"Thank you," Irene says. "You are a great lady for finishing your reading. You deserve a rest after such hard work. And a piece of dark chocolate when you wake up."

I kiss Mamaleh's forehead, then Irene helps me move her to the bedroom. Her slippers drag across the carpet, one foot slowly but surely passing the other. When I brace my hand under her elbow for support, I smell baby powder under her armpits. She's shivering.

"Your fingers are like icicles," I tell her, worried about her poor circulation.

"So turn up the heat, Heidi. Does it have to be Chanukah to get some heat in this house?"

"You're a legend," I tell her when we settle her in bed. "I love you."

It doesn't take long before she dozes off to sleep. I stay until I hear the hum of her snoring.

CHAPTER 33

Irene

October 2023

I remove a package of three crackers and cheese from the pocket of my sweater and munch as Mamaleh rests. The old woman's eyes flutter. She occasionally moans, not too loud, but still the sound frightens me. Dear God, I pray she is not having bad dreams. I worry that reading her tablet to us week after week brought back memories that should have stayed locked inside her. I only want to be a good caregiver, to make sure she is always safe and at peace. To me, she's like my own mommy. To lose both of her parents must have been so hard for her. A crime. Thank the Lord, my *nanay* and *tatay* are alive and can still take care of Winston. For how long, I don't know.

When Mamaleh is more settled, I go to the kitchen to begin dinner and start the laundry. Today I need to clean her bathroom and mop the kitchen floor. There are no real breaks in this job. It's go, go, go all the time. I've got to give Mamaleh her medicines several times a day, bathe her, not in the tub, just with a sponge, take her to the toilet, get her into and out of bed, help her walk, sit, and occasionally stand. Whenever she calls me, I'm right there at her side. That's my job. She doesn't need to know that my tooth aches. The guava leaf tea is not making the pain go away, though I would never tell Heidi that. She doesn't like to admit that dental insurance on my salary is impossible. But I refuse to go back to working at a residential facility for old people. During the pandemic, personal protective equipment was so terrible in those places. Sometimes our employers told us to reuse PPE that was intended for single use. Honestly, I don't know where I will work or live when my work on Maple Drive comes to an end. Maybe the Lord will take care of me and Winston like he took care of Mamaleh in the DP camp. I pray every Sunday in church for the Lord's help.

About a month ago, one hazy afternoon when Heidi was at the pickleball courts—where else would that girl be?—the strangest thing happened. Mamaleh asked me what I planned to do after she was gone. "No, no," I remember saying. I'm so superstitious. "Don't talk like that. What will be, will be." But Mamaleh shook her head. I can still hear her saying, "Irene, you have a son to take care of. You have parents. I won't be here forever."

I felt uncomfortable with what Mamaleh was telling me. I am her caregiver, but now she was trying to take care of me. I squeezed her hand. "Don't worry, Mamaleh. I'll find a place to live and a new job. Rest now. Don't worry about me. The Lord will look after me."

Instead of resting her head on the pillow, she pushed herself up and said, "You think I am an old lady who doesn't notice what's going on. I know when you are in pain, Irene. I know a toothache when I see it. I know you can't afford the dentist. It's hard enough to save money to send back home for your family. I see things. I hear you talking to your family on the phone. I see tears in your eyes when you hang up."

"No, no," I said again. I didn't want to upset her or be disrespectful. "My son is fine. My parents are healthy."

Then about a week later, when Heidi dropped off some grapes for Mamaleh, I had the shock of my life. The three of us were on the sofa in the living room having tea in the afternoon. The house was filled with the sweet smell of my apple cake, fresh from the oven. Mamaleh's hand shook as she lifted the teacup to her mouth.

"I want you to hear this when we are all together," she said. She stopped for a second, then went on. "I've decided to give this house to Irene." Heidi and I looked at each other, not sure how to respond.

"I want to die knowing that Irene is taken care of and she can bring her son to Canada."

Maybe Mamaleh was overtired, I thought. She must be confused. Did she have a stroke? I touched her forehead to see if she had fever, but her head was cool.

Heidi scooted more closely to Mamaleh, assuring her not to worry, that she would make sure that I was looked after. "Irene will be fine. I promise," Heidi told her mother.

Mamaleh shook her head. "No, no. I want her son to come to live with her here, in this house. He should be with his mother. I know about these things. They will live on Maple Drive."

"Let's talk about this later," Heidi said. "I'm going to be late for my game."

"You and your games, Heidi. I've made up my mind. You and all the grandchildren will be fine. Your father and I did well. There's enough for all of you. But I want to know that Irene and her son are comfortable too."

Nobody else was in the room with us. Just the old woman, her daughter, and me. I didn't take what Mamaleh said seriously. Elderly people hallucinate. Their brains become foggy. Mamaleh was likely showing signs of dementia typical in old age. I was touched, but I felt sorry for her confusion.

"Get my lawyer on the phone," Mamaleh told Heidi. I could tell she was agitated. "Right now. Tell her to change my will. Irene will inherit my house on Maple Drive. It needs a lot of repairs, but the foundation is solid. And call my lawyer before you run off to play that game. What is it called again? Pickle Jar?"

Instead of arguing with Mamaleh, Heidi reached for her phone, turned her back to her mother, and appeared to call the lawyer. She said, "That's right. It's my mother's wish to give her house on Maple Drive to her caregiver, Irene Santos. Yes, my mother is in good health today, of sound mind and body. No, she's not in any way delusional. This is what she really wants."

"Heidi, tell my lawyer to revise my will today," Mamaleh said in the background. "And send us the new will. Fax it over. I want to sign it before it's too late."

"Fax! Who has a fax machine these days?" Heidi laughed. "Nobody faxes anymore. We use our devices, you know, our computers and our phones."

"Then give me your phone, Heidi. Let me speak to the lawyer myself."

I could see that Mamaleh was getting upset so I patted her arm to calm her down.

"Oops," Heidi said. "The lawyer just hung up. She must be busy now, but I'll call her later today and have the revised will couriered to you. I promise."

I always knew that Heidi's promise was not for real. It was just her way to calm down Mommy. Heidi wanted Mommy not to worry about me. She wanted her to be at peace. That's what I want for the old woman too.

Two days after Mamaleh asked Heidi to change the will and give the house on Maple Drive to me, Mommy began to show signs that the end was not far off. Her skin was pale, sort of bluish. When I touched her face, it was cold. Her eyes were half open. She slept more and didn't respond when I spoke to her. I could hardly get her to eat. One meal a day at most. She wouldn't touch the sweet treats I made for her.

Heidi sat next to Mommy's bed, holding her hand while checking messages on her phone. The dings never seemed to stop. On the third afternoon Heidi stood up, kissed Mamaleh's forehead, and announced that she needed some fresh air. She promised to be back in a few minutes. I gave Heidi a stern look and shook my head at her. Was she crazy, leaving Mommy now? But Heidi grabbed her paddle and trotted out the front door. From the window I saw her swivel around, as if she had forgotten something. The door squeaked as she pushed it open. Heidi raced up the steps to Mamaleh's room. She bent over and whispered, "I love you."

Mamaleh blinked. I told her to rest. "You've done what you need to do," I said. As soon as Heidi pulled the front door shut for the second time, Mamaleh exhaled a strong whoosh of air.

One minute she was with us, and the next minute the Lord delivered her to heaven.

CHAPTER 34

Heidi

October 2023

Why did she die when I stepped away from her beside? Maybe she wanted to spare me the finality of her departure. Or she recognized her imminent death and accepted it. I'll never know the answer. At least Irene was with her. She didn't die alone. Yet I have regrets. Plenty of them. I should have asked her to forgive me for playing too much pickleball and not bringing her enough green grapes. I should have asked her to forgive me for ignoring my younger brother, Ian, and abandoning him at the park. I should have asked her to forgive me for not remarrying, for moving away from Maple Drive, for not being a better daughter.

On the flip side, I never said that I forgave her for the long silence she maintained about her past. Until Covid I lived without a family history. I never said that I forgave her for losing the photos of her birth family. What happened to all those pictures she guarded so fiercely? I'll never see how I resemble my grandmother who died in the attic. It's odd to go through life without a single image of my ancestors. It's as if they never existed. Of course I could have said that I'm grateful she survived, though the photos didn't. Yes, I wish I'd told her that. Nor did I say a final thank-you. Thank you for all you taught me. Thank you for your shtetl wisdom. Thank you for taking care of me. Thank you for being you. I regret that I never spoke those words to my mother.

I sit shiva for her, marking the seven days of mourning after her burial. Her house on Maple Drive is filled with family, neighbours, and community members coming to express their sympathy. My three sons join me for the nightly prayers. My grandchildren ask questions about their great-grandmother in between sandwiches, cake, and soft drinks. Ian has returned from Calgary where he is a dentist. Throughout the shiva, he sits on a low chair reserved for the immediate family. I place the photo albums from our childhood on the coffee table near him, a record of our parents' valiant determination to start over in Canada. Flipping through the cellophane-wrapped pages with him, I'm struck by how much Ian looks like my father. The bushy eyebrows and receding hairline are identical. I pause on a snapshot of Ian and Daddy both wearing the same blue baseball jerseys and baseball hats. That photo must have been taken the summer Daddy coached Ian's North Toronto baseball team. They're standing on the baseball diamond at home plate, likely after winning the game. Daddy's arm is draped around Ian's shoulder in a perfect father-and-son moment.

I thumb through all the other albums we have of us as kids, but I can't find a photo of my father and me that is like that snapshot of Ian and Daddy. I remember all those summer weekends they devoted to baseball. They would travel beyond Toronto for games, stop at McDonalds for dinner on the way home, then watch more baseball on television when they finally got here. On the nights that we ate dinner together, Ian and my father talked about major league baseball trades and which teams had the best pitcher. Once, Daddy and Ian went to New York on a father-son road trip to see the Yankees play a home game at Yankee stadium.

"You and Daddy really bonded over baseball," I say to Ian during the shiva.

"Were you jealous?"

"I guess so. Between his dental practice, his real estate investments, and baseball, I didn't spend as much time with him as you did. I think he loved you more than he loved me."

"Not true. His busy thing was just the way he kept himself in the present."

"You might be right. I once asked Daddy if he missed his mother and father. He wouldn't talk about them, but he did say the people who gave birth to you are always with you. It doesn't matter how long they're in your life, whether you knew them well or didn't know them at all. Their blood runs in you. That's an unbreakable bond."

Ian diverts his eyes to the street, then puts the family photo album on his lap and skips back to the photo of him and Daddy on the baseball diamond. "He was a good father," he says. "I got lucky."

Throughout the seven days of shiva, Irene remains in the house, helping serve food, doing dishes, and vacuuming the crumbs from the carpet. The passing of Mamaleh is a huge loss for her too. I'm not sure where she'll go when the shiva is over. Perhaps she'll help prepare the house for my son Simon and his family to move in. I hope that she continues to assist people who are dying. The Allen family is indebted to her for the care she selflessly bestowed on Mamaleh up until her last breath.

I'm elated that some picklers attend my mother's funeral. Others come to the shiva to see me. Their messages of condolence flood our WhatsApp site, though I wish they didn't feel obligated to provide a shiva meal. I can always order food, and Irene can prepare it. She will never let us go hungry.

[Joanne] We are family in fun times so we must also be family in times of grief. I'm happy to organize a shiva meal for Heidi and family. Let me know if you want to contribute

[Liz] I'm so sorry for your loss, Heidi. I'm happy to help serve a shiva meal

[Jackie] FYI. Details about the funeral for Heidi's mother Shayna Allen are on the Steeles Memorial website. I'm going. I'm in for the shiva meal too

[Lisa] Oh no. My deep, deep condolences, Heidi

[Arnold] My condolences to u and yr family, Heidi. May her memory be a blessing

[Ron] So sorry for your loss. Wishing you a long life

[Rachel] Sorry for your loss, Heidi. Never the right time to lose a loved one.

[Jim] My sincere condolences

And on it goes. So many kind words from the picklers. I'm overwhelmed.

[Jackie] Just a reminder for our next group lunch on October 21. If u have a pickleball game scheduled that day, just come afterward. All welcome. Sorry Heidi won't be able to join us. She's still in a period of mourning. This gathering will be our largest. Oh, someone cancelled and can't bring drinks. Can anyone else step up? Water is fine. Also need chairs

[Jackie] What a great lunch with all of u. So much fun to share food. We are a community. Sorry Heidi could not be with us

[Ron] I feel all of u in my heart. Thank u for lovely lunch. Heidi, you were missed

I read the posts several times, conceding that the picklers who play at the courts on Maple Drive are the extended Canadian family I never had, a chosen family that Mamaleh couldn't grasp. A family created by choice was as strange to her as chicken soup without matzo balls.

And we stay together by choice too.

CHAPTER 35

Irene

November 2023

I stay in Mommy's house once the shiva is over. Where am I going to go now that my full-time job is gone? Don't forget, I say to myself. You are needed here. Who else is going to get the house ready for Simon and his family to move in? What a mess. Mamaleh never threw anything away. How could Heidi believe that her mother lost those photos she brought from Europe when the old woman rarely parted with even the silliest things, like twist ties? Look at this place. Every room is packed with stuff. The kids' rooms still have their school desks in them. Their assignments are crammed into the drawers. Their clothes hang in the closets. It will take months to clear out all this junk.

I used to ask Mamaleh what she wanted to keep and what she wanted to toss out. I told her we could start sorting through items room by room and then arrange for the discarded things to go to Goodwill. All she needed to do was to say what should go to Heidi, Ian, the boys, and the great-grandchildren. Let's make a start on this, I kept suggesting. Let's do it while you are still strong enough to make decisions.

"No. Absolutely not," she said one afternoon. "A tea, if you would be so kindly, and a *bissel* of something, maybe a cookie." Then Mommy shook her head back and forth. "Why does Heidi need to know?"

She closed her eyes and pressed her lips together, like a zipped purse. I didn't know what she was talking about. Maybe she was unhappy because she didn't have an answer to her own question. Mommy usually knew everything. But on that day she sounded confused.

"I never wanted Heidi to see the family photos because nothing will bring back the dead. Not grief, not anger. I've said enough about Heidi's grandmother Miriam in my tablet. She doesn't need to know more. We should only talk about what will bloom, not about things that are dead."

Then, about a month later, when her health was running away fast, Mamaleh told me to go to the basement. Under the steps there was a storage area. "Take a flashlight," she said. "I can't go with you. My legs don't like steps anymore. But look in the storage area. You'll find a folder with photos and legal documents, things that we brought from the DP camp in Germany to Canada. Get them for me."

I rummaged around in the basement but couldn't find anything. When I told Mamaleh the bad news, she closed her eyes and then remembered that her husband, Hal, had moved everything upstairs because he was afraid of flooding in the basement.

"Go look in my bedroom closet, Irene. There's an opening to the attic in the ceiling of the closet. We used the space to store things we wanted to keep hidden. Be careful not to fall."

"You'll need to come with me," I said, and helped her climb the stairs so she could tell me where to look. I propped her against the pillows of her bed. Heidi was playing pickleball that afternoon on indoor courts east of Toronto. We had time to search for the photos and documents before she'd likely swing by to see Mamaleh on her way home. I moved Mommy's clothes to one side of the closet. I found a ladder and pushed open the crawl space. The smell of mildew hit me in the face. Dust and dirt from the attic floor covered my hands. I heard the scampering of mice as I hoisted myself into the unfinished space. Only one heavy plastic container with a tightfitting lid sat in the corner. When I opened it, I found a bulging folder of pictures and brought it to her. She pulled out the photos, held them up one by one, and told me who each person was. I took a pencil and paper to make a list of their names.

"This is my brother, Mendl, on the day of his bar mitzvah. After the war he was sent to a labour camp in Russia with my father. They died there. That is my grandmother Ruth, the photographer. And this is my mother, Miriam." She was wearing a floppy hat on an angle so it blocked one corner of her face. But her main features were noticeable, like her big smile.

Several photos remained on Mamaleh's lap. "There are two more," I said. "What about this one?" I handed her a picture of a young woman and man. They were pressed together so tightly that the blade of a knife couldn't slide between them. She was wearing a strand of pearls close to her throat. A crucifix hung from his neck. Surprised, I asked: "Is that your mother?"

When Mamaleh didn't respond, I took the photo and peeked at the back of it. The writing was too faint to read. With a flashlight from the drawer of Mamaleh's beside table, I lit up their names: *Miriam and Casimir, 1929.*

Mamaleh grabbed the photo from my hand, ripped it down the middle, as if to separate Miriam and Casimir forever, and dropped the two pieces of the photo into the wastebasket near her bed. "*Feh,*" she said.

She picked up the last photo but didn't speak as she fixed her eyes on it.

"Who were they?" I asked, leaning over to see the snapshot of a youthful girl and a handsome man in the back of a pickup truck. "Where was this photo taken?"

"That's me and the intern from the hospital in Germany. It was taken on the weekend we went to the training farm. I'm wearing his wool scarf. It was cold on that truck."

"Do you remember his name? I'll add it to the list."

"Herman," she said. "His name is Herman Petersen."

"And this. What's this envelope here at the bottom?" I didn't know how I was going to keep all this stuff straight.

"I think it's Heidi's birth certificate from the DP camp. You can throw it away too because I made her another one, which she has somewhere."

"Okay. Don't worry, Mommy. Everything will be the way you want it." I put all of it back in the folder and then glance at the two pieces of the ripped photo in the wastepaper basket. Both halves, I decide, will be saved too.

"After I'm gone, you can give these things to Heidi. Tell her that I never wanted to show her the photos because I didn't want her to feel sad for relatives that she would never know. Nothing's worse than having missing people hang around in your life. Best to leave them behind."

I'm a loyal person who follows orders. If Mamaleh wanted me to wait until after she was gone to give Heidi the photos, that's what I planned to do. The right moment comes about three weeks later. Mommy had passed by then, and Heidi tells me she's ready to start cleaning up the house.

"I have something Mamaleh left for you," I say to her after lunch. "She asked me to wait to give you a very special folder after she was no longer with us. Do you want it now?"

"Sure. You can show it to me, but I have a game soon in Woodbridge so it'll have to be quick."

I bring her the folder and spread the photos across the dining room table. I think she might cry when she sees her family for the first time so I bring a box of tissues with me. But I don't notice a single tear on her cheeks.

"I made a list of the people in the photos, Heidi. Do you want to read it?"

"No. I don't have time this afternoon." She bends over the table and stares at one photo, the picture of her grandmother Miriam. "I do look like her, don't I? So that's where I got my pointy chin."

"There is another document in an envelope in the folder too."

"Another time. Just keep all this stuff tied together. Thank you, Irene."

I hear her car lurch out of the driveway. Bundling up everything, I thank the Lord that Heidi has finally seen her grandmother's face. I hope Mommy is happy for this in heaven. I doubt that Heidi will ever stop playing pickleball long enough to finish the final job of cleaning up the house and throwing things away.

I'm not at all surprised when, a few days later, Heidi asks me to stay for several more months to continue helping her. She mentions there's a woman in her pickleball group who is looking for someone to care for her father, who is in his final stage of a terminal illness.

"You know, Irene," she says. "You'd make a great death doula when your job on Maple Drive is finished."

"A what? I never heard the word *doula* before. Did you make it up?"

"Of course not. Birth doulas or coaches have been around for a while, and now some families are hiring death doulas to assist someone who's close to death by providing physical support and to be there emotionally for the ill person and the family. Kind of like an end-of-life coach or a death midwife. It's what you did for Mamaleh and us."

"That's a career?"

"Yup. There are training workshops, classes, and some sort of certification. Let me know if you're interested. Got to run. My game's starting soon."

Off Heidi goes, always in fast motion. From the window I watch her hop in her car and speed away. How does she come up with these crazy ideas? A death doula? In my culture we don't need end-of-life coaches or death midwives. We care for dying people in our family without waiting to be asked, because of our faith. We know the Almighty is watching over us. No going to classes or getting certified is required for the job. Just love and devotion.

CHAPTER 36

Jonathan

November 2023

Heidi calls me in early November to say that she misses playing pickleball and wants to get back into it. I haven't heard from her in the month since her mother died. She asks if I would be interested in giving her a few lessons before the snow flies. Sure. I'm agreeable, but I tell her it would be far easier if she joins Oakridge. The indoor courts have just been resurfaced, and they're well maintained. No loose debris to trip on. What could be better? No, no, she protests. Oakridge is out of the question. The place reminds her too much of her first lesson with Sylvia there. When she doesn't offer any details about Sylvia's whereabouts, I let it go.

The last thing I want to do is upset Heidi. From the sound of her voice, which is uncharacteristically subdued, I'm guessing her mother's death really took a chunk out of her. I never met the old woman, but Heidi once mentioned that she was a Holocaust survivor. Tough as nails and extremely philanthropic. She apparently made large donations to all kinds of organizations in the city. Heidi must have inherited her mom's determination. When she fixates on something, like improving in pickleball, she won't let go. The irony is, she doesn't play like that. Something happens when she steps on the court. She wilts, often sabotaging her own game. I don't get it.

We agree to meet on Maple Drive the following weekend, if the weather gods don't send us rain, high winds, or early snow. As it happens, we're in luck on Sunday morning—the courts are dry. But the air is cold, the kind of cold that makes you wish you were spending the day under a weighted blanket watching football. The park is empty when we arrive. No, I spot one pissed-off teenager at the edge of the baseball diamond, dragging his puppy away from a mound of dirt. Poor dog.

As soon as I greet Heidi, my jaw drops. She seems like a different person—more reserved, almost quiet. Judging from her gaunt face, she's lost a lot of weight. It doesn't help that her hair is super short and, to be honest, unflattering.

"Hey. Good to see you." I squeeze her hands, but she makes no effort to return the friendly gesture. Sometimes you expect a show of appreciation when you're trying your best to connect with someone. Nope, wasn't happening this time. She nods and pulls the hood of her jacket over her head.

"Thank you for coming, Jonathan. It's been so long since I played that I feel like a beginner again. God forbid."

"C'mon, Heidi. Starting from scratch isn't that terrible." I want to reassure her, though I understand her frustration. Nobody likes giving up hard-won gains. "Trust me. Your potential isn't measured by the height of the peak you reach playing the game. Potential is demonstrated by how far you had to climb to get there. And you're continuing to make incredible progress."

"It's a bit different when you're my age. I'm running out of time, if you haven't noticed."

"Alright, Methuselah. Let's go."

"Ha-ha! But you do know that Methuselah was a guy."

"Okay, you one-upped me with that one. I never thought about the gender of Methuselah."

"Now you know. Just remember, I'm a woman, and don't forget it."

I smile, as if I could forget Heidi's gender for a split second. I'm pleased that her assertiveness is making a comeback. It could be good for her game.

Shortly after we start dinking, the boredom factor kicks in. I could hit the ball back and forth in soft strokes like this forever, and so could Heidi. My gaze shifts to the street, hoping—praying—that Sylvia will walk by. I imagine her turning into the park and strolling down the path to the courts. Her pickleball gear is in a gym bag slung across her shoulder. Her blue braided headband holds back that streaky blond hair I adore. She waves. Can I join you? More than anything, those are the words I want to hear—*Can I join you?*—but she isn't there to speak to us. I do see a woman passing by the park, but it's only a mirage, an illusion in my head of the real Sylvia.

I'm still fantasizing about her when Heidi hits a perfect dink to me. The ball bounces at my feet. I scoop it up with a little too much force and watch it sail over Heidi's right shoulder. She shuffles backward in that direction to grab the ball out of the air, extending her arm, and yells, "I've got it." And then—oh no, don't tell me—just as her paddle contacts the swirling ball, she falls to the ground. Fuck! It's my fault. I feel as guilty as hell. What if she broke her wrist or hip? And she's barely finished mourning her mother. An injury is the last thing she needs now.

Before I reach the other side of the court, she's standing. Despite the tumble, there's Heidi upright, brushing a dead leaf off her jacket. She's not screaming in pain. Blood is not gushing from her nose or anywhere else. She has no missing teeth that I can see. Heidi is so composed that I wonder if she's in shock. The fall didn't seem to register in any obvious way.

"I'm fine, Jonathan," she says. "Still breathing. Let's play."

"Hang on, Heidi. You might have broken something. Can you move your wrist? What about your elbow? I have a great physiotherapist downtown. You should see him before you play again."

"No way I'm going downtown for physio." But when she tries to swing her paddle, she grabs her right shoulder and scrunches her face in pain.

"You've got an injury, sweetheart. You need to go home, rest, and ice your shoulder."

"First, I'm not your sweetheart and stop patronizing me. Second, I've spent a month sitting and doing nothing. Let's dink for a few more minutes. Then I'll go home and take care of my shoulder. No worries."

I don't have the nerve to disappoint her when she looks so gutted. Thirty days of heavy grieving has taken a toll on Heidi. I can't pile more shit on her now. "Okay," I say, "but only if you use your left hand. I'm not risking more injury to your right shoulder or my reputation as an injury-conscious coach."

"Are you serious? That's totally absurd. I can't do anything with my left hand, and anyway, this is not about you. Everyone knows you're a smart coach."

"Flattery will get you nowhere, Ms. Know-It-All. It's left-handed play or nothing."

Heidi gives me one of her snarky looks and hesitates for less than a minute. When she finally transfers the paddle from her right to her left hand, I'm relieved, but also stunned. She's typically stubborn as hell, but she's more vulnerable today, more desperate to return to pickleball, more obsessed, like a pit bull with a frigging bone. I tell her that lots of people use both hands to play or switch arms after an injury. Sometimes players even switch the paddle to their nondominant hand in the heat of the moment when a shot is coming at them, though, I caution her, it's unadvisable. Those players never develop the full range of skills with their dominant arm.

She listens and then sighs. "Okay, fuck it. I'm ready to begin again."

It's not easy for her or for me. She misses almost every shot, stamps her foot, kicks the ball, shouts curses across the net, and generally resists putting in the effort it takes to switch arms. We're stuck. On the bench I remind Heidi of Einstein's famous quote, which I often use with clients. "The definition of insanity is doing the same thing over and over and expecting a different result." When Heidi doesn't comment, I add, "You've got an opportunity here. Discomfort is a good thing. It'll improve your game, even accelerate your growth, if you stop running from it."

"Bullshit, Mr. Nice Guy. And FYI, there's no evidence that Einstein ever said that."

"Okay, Heidi. All I can say is stop avoiding discomfort. Try playing with your left hand. I mean really try. Be a beginner again. It won't kill you. Take the risk. Make mistakes. You know, dear, perfectionism doesn't correlate with improved performance. Get comfortable with being uncomfortable and imperfect."

"Stop lecturing me, Jonathan, and if you call me dear or sweetheart one more time…" She packs up her court shoes and gets up to leave. I try to catch her eye, but what I get back is a detached glare.

CHAPTER 37

Sylvia

November 2023

I feel broken. Hollow. I'm beginning to realize after all these days locked in my study that there isn't anything I can do to fix this mess. The holes in my life will always be there. They are permanent. There was a time when I thought Danny would be enough. I thought that for years. I loved him. I still do. He can be generous and giving, like the time he brought me an orchid because he knows I adore plants and flowers. We've become so tightly bonded together after all these years in a traumatic marriage, but I don't want to be controlled in everything I do anymore. I woke up today with a crushing sense of wrongness, of shame for all the hurt I've caused. I feel so guilty. Heidi is probably worrying about me this very minute. Of course she is. With that mother of hers, it's second nature.

And then there's Jonathan. He's always helpful and seems so concerned about me. That heart tattoo on his arm reflects his inner generosity. I knew that from the first time I met him at Oakridge. I don't deserve his kindness, or his love. I feel guilty that I've let him down, not to mention Joe. Such a convenient escape when I needed him. Okay, there's my sister. She means well, but she never really understood what was happening between Danny and me. No, maybe she did, but it doesn't matter now. None of these people matter now. No, that's not true. The loss of Jonathan and what we had together is too painful to bear.

I'm crumpled on the floor. My whole body feels like it's turning inside out. I want to make myself smaller and smaller until I disappear. I don't understand the person I've become. God, Danny must hate me. I hate me. I was never this kind of person before. I try not to think of our worst days, but the memories crowd into my head. All those fights. I have nothing else to think about. I should have told someone about his tirades. A professional, I mean. The punches, the punishment. That's what my sister said. Talk to a professional. If only I had some sleeping pills now so I could sleep endlessly. When he brought me something to eat yesterday, I pushed the tray away. Then he came close to me and squeezed my hand. I thought he was reassuring me that everything would be good again between us soon. Instead, he squeezed my hand tighter and tighter until I screamed out. He said he would stop bringing me food if I didn't tell him who really gave me the money and what I had done with him. When he left the room and locked the door, my hurting fingers grasped the handle. I bit down hard on my lips and twisted the handle. No movement. Then I let it go. I'm a prisoner here.

Sitting on the sofa bed, I curl up and wrap my arms around my knees to stop from trembling. I need a mission, some sort of exit strategy. Looking across the room, I wonder if that curtain rod will support me if I suspend myself from the curtains. It shouldn't be hard. I'm light as a feather now. But maybe not a great idea. There are other ways. Kate Spade hanged herself with a red scarf tied to the doorknob in her bedroom. Nylon or silk? On the subject of fabric, the curtains in here sure do need to be washed. What's the point of sheers if they're dingy grey instead of snow white?

CHAPTER 38

Heidi

December 2023

I'm not in the habit of reading obits every morning. It's too damn depressing. Somebody recently told me that life expectancy in Canada is, in fact, trending downward. Which means we'd better squeeze in as many games of pickleball as we can now because we'll have fewer years in the future to perfect our topspin. Thank you, Covid. We may also need to squish games in between the increasing number of funerals, shivas, and celebrations of life we will no doubt be attending. Just yesterday I went to a celebration of life in a public library to commemorate a deceased friend's love of books. Every attendee received a bookmark with a smiling photo of her on it. I remember those red-framed glasses she was wearing in the photo and her amused eyes. Now I only have her image on a bookmark tucked into *Hello Beautiful*, a bestselling novel that she'll never have the chance to read. I miss her already.

On this bleak December morning, while indulging in a second cup of coffee, I mindlessly scan the death notices in the newspaper, too lazy to load the dishwasher or put away the milk. My eyes flit from the top of the obit page to the bottom, noting a few details about the deceased. One was the linchpin of the Toronto Irish community;

another was a generous, honourable man, well respected in the investment world; and a third was a woman who served as the chief of anesthesiology at a rural hospital, remembered fondly as "one of a kind." The words in the death notices often fall short of a full expression of love, despite the earnest intentions of the writers. Yet they convey a genuine sense of respect in a way that honours the dead. Isn't that what obituaries are supposed to do? I would have thought so, until I stumble on a tiny death notice in the lower right corner of the page.

SYLVIA GREENE

September 10, 1955—December 5, 2023

Died suddenly in Toronto. In lieu of flowers, donations may be made to the Toronto Humane Society.

No! Could that be our Sylvia? It must be a different Sylvia Greene. The name is common enough. A quick scan on Facebook indicates several women with that name. One lives in Ottawa and another in Dundas, Ontario. Neither one is our Toronto Sylvia. I drop my head on the table and feel my shoulders shaking. It must be her, but is that the entire obit? I pinch my eyes closed, too angry to cry. Why is there no information on her funeral or the burial ground? Where's the photo of the beautiful Sylvia? Where will the shiva be held or are we expected just to show up on Shoremount with prayer books in hand and start reciting the Mourner's Kaddish for her on their driveway? And why should donations be made to the Toronto Humane Society? Who thought that one up? Sylvia liked animals, but she was not what you'd call an ardent animal lover. She adored plants and gardens. But she didn't go out of her way to swoon over a cockapoo or adopt a guinea pig. A cat, maybe, though she never mentioned having a pet. Donations would be better directed to the Toronto Botanical Garden. Also absent from the obit are the typical references to a beloved husband, a cherished sister, or adored nephews and nieces left behind. Sylvia's death notice is so spare and devoid of people that it's an affront to her warmth, her care for others, and her devotion to her family, friends, and former colleagues. I'm livid.

My hand trembles on my coffee cup as I scan the two measly sentences again. The injustice of it. When I take another sip, I choke and spew brown liquid onto the table in the vicinity of my phone. I wipe the screen on the sleeve of my turtleneck sweater and scroll to my WhatsApp page, flicking away the coffee that dribbles down my chin. I'm a complete mess. The obit is so outrageous.

[Heidi] Did anyone see the death notice for Sylvia in the paper today or am I imagining that she died? The obit is an insult to her life, her personhood, her very existence

[Lisa] Just saw it. It's for real. How did she die?

[Ron] Don't question how she died. Celebrate her instead

[Liz] Maybe she was murdered. Should we contact the police?

[Joanne] To say what? What evidence do we have? Let her rest in peace. We don't need to know

[Liz] We need to do something. Justice should be served

[Jonathan] She loved pickleball. That's what we know. That's how we should celebrate her life

[Heidi] She was battered by her husband. Didn't you see her face, those bruises. All that makeup she wore to cover the welts

[Joanne] But do you have any proof her husband caused the bruises? Be careful what you say if you don't want to get sued for libel. But I know where you're coming from. Intimate partner abuse is more common than you think. Even in our hood

[Lisa] True, but Sylvia wouldn't want us to push this any further

[Ron] Her husband isn't going to cooperate. It might be a cover up, but better to let it go. We're just her friends. We don't have any personal info about her life outside of pickleball. I don't even know if she had a will. Why would I?

[Heidi] No, you wouldn't. So OK. Let's meet at the courts on Maple Drive today at noon to discuss how to respond. That's where I feel closest to Sylvia

[Liz] Yup. C u there

The snow piles up on my windowsill. Wetness clouds my eyes. What a tragic life Sylvia had. I go to her house and knock on the door. There's no answer. The curtains are drawn on the first floor. I look up to the second floor. The large window is bare. No lights are on in the house. No car in the driveway. No signs of life. I look at that large window again. I imagine svelte Sylvia hanging from the gauzy curtain that used to be there. She wouldn't do something horrible like that. Or would she? Suicide is always mysterious. The how and why are often left unresolved.

At the courts we bunch together, shivering, clutching each other for support. I feel robbed. Not only is Sylvia gone, I don't even know what happened to her. Yet nobody wants to press for an investigation. Danny Greene would likely block any attempt to dig deeper into Sylvia's death. He already stopped our earlier efforts to contact her. He'd deny any accusation of foul play. And Sylvia wouldn't want us to delve into their private life together. She'd feel violated if she knew we were snooping in her personal affairs. The group decides not to take further action.

Yet we all agree that we must do something to remember Sylvia and honour her. Back at my condo I bustle around. I put my kitchen and dining room chairs in a circle and I pour chamomile tea for everyone, pressing the warm cups into their hands. Then I stop. I'm about to cry, and once the tears flow, I won't be able to recover. Sylvia, the most repressed woman I know, would be appalled if I lost control in front of our pickleball buddies because of her.

"Hey," Lisa says to break the silence, "whatever happened to Sylvia's blue headband. You know, that braided one you and Liz found on the court. Do you still have it?"

"I've got it." I go into my bedroom and pull the hair accessory from my top drawer, where I keep precious things.

We pass around Sylvia's headband. Whoever is holding it can speak without interruption. She is most remembered for her score-keeping prowess in pickleball, no mean feat. When players couldn't remember whether they had five points or eight, Sylvia always knew. She could have won the Fields Medal in mathematics if she'd been mentored properly, but she wasn't. Danny boy made sure of that. Numbers were Sylvia's friends. Strong math skills were her ticket to employment. Oh, she was also kind and considerate, asking frequently about our ill mothers or the schools our grandchildren attended. Listening to these memories of Sylvia, I think how superficially we knew Sylvia, and yet how deeply she penetrated our hearts. Mine the deepest, I suspect, because she was the sister I never had.

When everyone departs, it's late in the afternoon. I leave the empty cups scattered around the living room. In my bedroom I wrap myself in a blanket and cry as quietly as I can, just in case Sylvia is somewhere close, listening to me. I don't want to make her sad if she can hear me. I hope wherever she is that she can't feel my despair. I would do anything, anything, to be able to get out of bed and hug her and say how much I miss her. I need to tell her that I'm so sorry that I couldn't save her. If she feels guilty about causing anyone pain, I want to tell her that I feel guilty too.

CHAPTER 39

Jonathan

January 2024

Sylvia, wherever you are, I want you to know this: I dream nightly of your face. In my daily life I coach a steady stream of eager pickleball players with the sound of your voice always in my head, as it is now. You were like a messenger from some urgent place, coaxing me to trust you, to share my feelings, to listen, instead of constantly advising, correcting, and teaching those desperate folks seeking my services. I've always been a coach, but never a lover. You taught me that intimacy is the opposite of power-tripping. I learned about emotional connection from you, Sylvia. Ironic, isn't it, that I don't even know how you died.

Heidi knew nothing about us. I don't think she ever figured out that we got together without her, away from pickleball and the courts. She is and will always be blinded by pickleball. She won't allow herself to see that there's life outside of the game and a world beyond Maple Drive. I know you felt close to Heidi, but, honestly, Sylvia, she wasn't a good fit for you. That preachy feminism of hers never did justice to the complexity of your situation or your feelings. We found that understanding together, Sylvia. Heidi could never accept you in the way that I do.

And Danny Greene. I'm devastated when I think about the abuse you experienced living with that monster. In my brief encounter with Danny boy—brief is an understatement given that he slammed the door in my face when I tried to bring you almond bark one day—I found him worse than I imagined. When he came to the door, he was cold, calculating, impolite, and physically unattractive. I can't begin to understand how you married him or stayed in that relationship as long as you did. Talk about the intimacy gap! You were never going to feel emotionally connected to him. You told me he never supported anything you tried to do.

Okay, sorry. I promised not to judge you or coach you. I do understand that you see yourself—I mean, you saw yourself—as a traditional woman who stands by her man, no matter what. I know you were afraid to leave him because you felt so isolated. Danny boy made sure of that. Your sister was no help. All you had was me. Sylvia, I wanted to be there for you. Night and day. To be your all. Of course I noticed the bruises on your face, but I didn't want to give Heidi the feminist satisfaction of discovering a real live case of intimate partner abuse. I wanted to help you in my own way. If anyone was going to save you, it was going to be me. In the end, both Heidi and I failed you.

Heidi can grieve with her pickleball network—a bunch of pickleball fanatics, if you ask me. I don't dare tell them about us. All my hard work to become the best and brightest pickleball coach in Toronto would vanish in a second. My women clients would desert me in droves. I do know that the pickleball players saw only a sliver of what you really are—were: a compassionate woman in search of a soul mate. Me. We matched perfectly because neither of us had children. We became each other's child. I was much closer to you than I was to my two previous wives. How disgusting that Danny blamed you for the lack of offspring. You were always going to be enough for me. No children required.

What happened to us? The turning point came one afternoon in, of all places, a swanky hotel. Do you remember that one not too far east of the courts on Maple Drive? The Novotel, I think it was. We spent lots of afternoons in hotels, always careful to pick different spots to avoid getting caught and to keep things spicy. We both got a kick out of the secrecy in our relationship, like we were sneaky lovers in a B-grade Hollywood movie. Novotel, however, was not a B-grade establishment. I booked a newly renovated, spacious room, which pleased you because Danny boy forced you to live in a disastrous dumpster of a house. I'd never let you live in such degrading conditions.

As soon as we arrived at the Novotel, we showered together. That was how we liked to begin. I soaped your bruised body and washed your hair, taking exquisite care to leave no traces of shampoo on your scalp. I wrapped you in a fluffy, luxurious towel and dried your long limbs, your breasts, under your arms, between your legs, until I could feel all the tension slowly being released from your body. When you said you were starving, I had room service deliver a steak sandwich, salad, and dessert for you, then fed you the chocolate mousse from a silver spoon, one creamy bite at a time. You almost purred with pleasure. I'll never forget that. I was happy too, until you turned over your right arm, and I looked more closely at the scratches piercing your skin. You pulled your arm away when I touched the deep red marks. These scratches did not resemble the kind of light scratches you give yourself accidentally in your sleep. The scratch marks looked like a tiger had dug its claws into you. I put down the spoon and pushed my chair away from you. I felt sick just looking at your mutilated skin. I stood up. I said, "Sylvia, you will not go back into that house. I can't let you. He's going to kill you. You are coming to live with me."

You shook your head and smiled. "I love you, dear Jonathan, but I can't leave Danny."

Something inside me snapped. I told you that unless you moved out, I couldn't keep seeing you—I'd break off our relationship. It was my way or the highway. If you cared about me, I told you in no uncertain terms, you'd ditch that brutal husband of yours. Remember, I've been married before. I know how to play hardball when I need to. When my first wife had an affair with her boss, I put the screws to her. Trust me, it didn't end well for her. And when you refused to leave Danny, I also called it quits. Just tell me, Sylvia: Was

I, a pickleball coach who didn't grow up in Forest Hill, somehow not good enough for you?

Obviously I knew you were trying to hurt me when you took up with that loser in the park. You became such a willing participant in a situation that made absolutely no sense. Your shenanigans with those roughnecks had nothing to do with them. Everything you did with them was about me. You were trying to punish me. I knew that. You tried to make me feel jealous so that I'd admit I was wrong to pressure you into leaving Danny. You tried to guilt me into taking you back. Maybe I should have, but I didn't. You were eating up my life, and I was eating up yours.

CHAPTER 40

Heidi

January 2024

In the weeks following the death of Mamaleh, I cried often and for no reason. Even now, reading is a struggle, though I carry books around—too many of them—wherever I go, knowing I won't open them. An essential part of me has slipped away. And just when I crave light, the sun decides to take a vacation. I'm stuck inside to avoid the soaking mix of ice pellets, snow, and rain pounding the windows. Even pickleball fanatics would be foolish to buck the elements to play outdoors. Yet, despite the disastrous weather, I receive notifications of outdoor games regularly on the Pickleball Organizer. Over one million pickleball dates across North America have been scheduled using the online organizer. How many of those dates become romantic attachments, I wonder, but then again, who's counting? My deceased mother is. She's likely keeping score in heaven. No word from Jonathan of late. Apparently, there's a pickleball coach at Triumph Sportsplex who is funnier, smarter, and a better player than Jonathan. Imagine that.

On many nights Mamaleh's voice keeps me company. I listen to her reading from her tablet and whisper, "You are not forgotten." One evening just before midnight, when I'm binging on my second bag of nacho chips as she reads on the video recording, I fantasize about making a pilgrimage to the attic where my grandmother met her death. I want to stand on the spot where she died. I want to crawl into the attic closet where Mamaleh clung to her mother's waist until she had no choice but to let go. I'd like to build a little shrine to my grandmother there, displaying her ankle-length silver fox coat, a few of her fashionable dresses, and a favourite hat. To be honest, I doubt any of these prized possessions still exist. If they do, it's unlikely I'd be able to find them. I don't even know if my grandmother's house is still standing. If by some miracle it is, would the owners invite me in? Do they know what happened in their attic? Do they care?

The nacho chips are finished. My nocturnal fantasies end, but not my disappointment. I'll never be able to honour my grandmother with a shrine. Mamaleh made sure of that. I can't find Szczniki, the Polish town she called her birthplace. I've combed several Polish town locators to find Szczniki, as well as the JewishGen Gazetteer, which lists towns in Central and Eastern Europe using present or former names. No luck. There's Szczytniki in west-central Poland and Slomniki in the south, but I have no way of knowing if Mamaleh's family lived in either one of them. I can only deduce that my wily mother invented the town of Szczniki. But I can't fathom why. If she thought it was important enough to keep a tablet documenting her earlier life, then why would she disguise such a detail as crucial as the name of her birthplace?

I'm beginning to question whether any of Mamaleh's tablet can be verified. Or maybe she was selective in her approach, cherry-picking the parts of her story that she was prepared to share and protecting the parts in which she still felt the most vulnerable. I'll never know her rationale because I have no one to ask. My brother removed himself from any involvement in the family saga long ago when he moved to Calgary and left me in charge. No one from Mamaleh's extended family is alive. Her brother, Mendl, who would have been close to a hundred years old now, died somewhere in Russia with their father. I don't know where or when.

I have only one person to question, and she's an unlikely source at that: Irene Santos. She became Mamaleh's confidante in the final years of her life and was closer to her in some respects than I was.

Today, while wrapping cups and saucers in newspaper and packing them in boxes, I ask her if Mamaleh ever divulged the real name of her birthplace. Irene stonewalls by pinning her eyes on a stain in the dining room carpet, so I try a different tactic.

"By the way, Irene, I'd like you to have some of Mamaleh's dishes," I say. "You took such good care of her, and I know she'd want you to have them."

"Thank you, but I can't take them," Irene says. "Mommy didn't want us to keep things from the past. Better to forget."

"Did she hide the name of her town from me? Just tell me. I have the right to know."

"Can you accept not knowing?" she says without flinching. "Mommy made me promise that I'd never tell you. She didn't want you to step your baby toe in Poland or her town. Too much blood on the ground over there. Too many secrets you don't need to know. That's what she always said. 'Heidi should never ever go there.'" Irene shakes her head.

I am angry as hell with Mamaleh for withholding such a crucial piece of information about her life from me. Irene's unwavering loyalty to my mother is just as infuriating. I frown at her, but she beams back a smile. "There's nothing wrong with missing pieces in a person's life, Heidi. Mommy wasn't trying to deceive you. She wanted to protect you."

I feel my hands shaking. A saucer slips out of my grip and breaks. Before Irene gets the broom, I pick up the porcelain shards to dispose of them, but the jagged edge of the broken saucer gashes my finger. Blood dribbles onto the carpet. "Fuck," I blurt out.

Irene is quick to draw a lesson from the accident. "You see, Heidi—Mommy is telling you not to go back there. Listen to her for once."

"Hmm. Maybe." I wrap an adhesive bandage around my finger and put the Poland question on hold for the time being.

In the following weeks I focus my attention exclusively on the chaos Mamaleh left behind. Dismantling a parent's house is a painful process, as anyone who has ever done it knows. There are so many decisions to make about the artwork on the walls, the handmade quilts on the beds, the racks of shoes in the closet, the cutlery in the dingy kitchen drawers. Each time I appraise an object of hers, I'm conflicted. If I trash it, I'm throwing away a piece of her. If I save it, I'm preserving her legacy. But for whom? Nobody wants Mamaleh's things. And she didn't care a fig about her legacy or how people remembered her once she was gone. God forbid her own daughter should know where she was born. Is that too much to ask?

Maybe. But a return to my birthplace in Germany is a different matter. It's certainly appropriate to want to see the hospital in the displaced persons camp where I entered the world. I call myself a Bergen-Belsen baby for a reason. My story begins there. But, for Mamaleh, the DP camp was an end as well as a beginning. Bergen-Belsen meant a rupture in the life she had known. She associated the DP camp with a forced departure from her Polish homeland, an exile her father imposed despite her protests. She never saw him again. I do understand that I was born at a transitional moment for my grieving parents, wracked no doubt with survivors' guilt. How lonely and different the DP camp must have felt in contrast to the happy shtetl where Mamaleh was born and raised. Her small town was steeped in tradition and overflowed with aunts, uncles, and cousins. Her view of the DP camp must have been tinged by memories of that irretrievable place and all that she lost. But for me, birth in the DP camp offered a clean slate, free of guilt and trauma. At least that's what my mother's long-maintained silence led me to believe.

Emptying the top drawer in her bedroom dresser this afternoon, I recognize that brown folder where she kept the few photos and documents she brought from Europe. The corners are tattered and the flap is crumpled. Irene must have tied the string around the folder to hold the deteriorating old thing together after Mamaleh died. I lift it out of the drawer, intending to take a fast peek at the photos before my pickleball game, but I can't undo the knot. I've bitten my nails to the quick and my arthritic fingers are useless. Fuck it. I'm going to be late. I shove the envelope back in the drawer.

I head off to Triumph Sportsplex, bombing up Highway 400 until traffic grinds to a standstill. A truck jackknifed about a kilometre ahead. Fuck, fuck, fuck. I'm trapped. My mind returns to Mamaleh's brown folder and the meagre remnants of her earlier life. What exactly is my duty to her past? That's the question I wrestle with as I sit immobilized on a road of frustrated drivers and revving engines. How can I honour her memories while keeping those memories and her past from consuming me? By the time I pull into the parking lot at Triumph twenty minutes later, I'm convinced that I need to see Bergen-Belsen for myself.

If Mamaleh chose silence to protect my brother and me from the catastrophic events defining her childhood, I'm striving to reverse that pattern, first by video-recording Mamaleh reading from her writing tablet, and then by making it available to my sons. They are now in a unique position to learn about their grandmother's past, a privilege my brother and I weren't given in our younger years. Perhaps Mamaleh agreed to make a video recording of her wartime experiences because she recognized the need to find a permanent resting place for her memories. Though she never said as much, she may have hoped that her grandchildren, the third generation of Holocaust survivors, would pass along her story to the fourth generation. My sons are free of course to decide whether they want to accept the Holocaust as part of their identities or to separate from it. The choice is completely theirs. No pressure, I tell them, when I invite each son to join me on my return voyage to Germany, which will feature a visit to the DP camp where their grandmother resuscitated her life after World War II and to the hospital where I was delivered.

On the next Shabbat I ask my eldest son, Josh, if he'd like to accompany me on the journey.

"Sure," he says. "Just let me know when you get there, and we can FaceTime. No worries. We'll do it."

My second son, Ben, responds to my invitation while carpooling his daughter to figure skating practice. "Great idea, Mom," he says.

"Tell me when you'll be there, and I'll set up a Zoom link. We don't all need to schlep to Germany to see decrepit buildings, do we?"

"Fine," I say to both sons. "Whatever." However, Simon, who's more invested in our family history, agrees to come with me. For him, Mamaleh's survival is emblematic of her tenacious strength. He wants to see where she tested that character trait and succeeded.

We visit Bergen-Belsen concentration camp during Simon's March break from teaching. The concentration camp is not far from the DP camp of the same name. Spring is late to arrive in Germany. I'm unprepared for the chilled air stinging my cheeks and stiffening my bare neck. The hoodless wool coat I'm wearing is totally wrong for the occasion. What was I thinking? I should have worn my down jacket with a fur-lined hood and also packed my plaid cashmere scarf.

Standing at the entry to the concentration camp, huddled against Simon to block the cold, I fear what awaits us. My lips mouth the words written on the stone entrance wall: *Bergen-Belsen 1940 bis 1945*. A sense of dread envelops me. My stomach cramps. Once we enter the former concentration camp grounds, there is an otherworldly stillness. The sound of the wind blowing through the high treetops and an eagle flapping its heavy wings—that's all I hear. Little of the camp structure remains. When British troops liberated the Bergen-Belsen camp and burned the living quarters to the ground to prevent the spread of illness, they left only the foundations of a few barracks, the remnants of a root cellar, and a water pit. I tug my coat more tightly around me as we continue to walk. We gasp at the sight of huge mounds of soil, which are mass graves where thousands of people were buried. Monuments dot the barren landscape. By the time we reach the symbolic gravestone commemorating Anne Frank and her sister, Margot, my breath is rushing in and out in spasmodic bursts. In that moment I stop thinking of Anne Frank as an icon. No, I'm here to mourn her as I would a childhood friend. The location of her body and her sister's is unknown, I soon discover.

Although the terrain of Bergen-Belsen is desolate, the ground where such inhumane events occurred still has the power to pull me in. I listen for the meek voices of the prisoners begging for water. I smell the stench of their bodies, sick with typhus, dysentery, and starvation. I see skeletal figures moving around in a daze, heads shaven. I can't absorb any more. My capacity to comprehend the horror reaches the point of saturation.

"Sorry, Simon," I say. "I'm tired. I'll wait for you in the café while you visit the Documentation Centre."

"Sure," he says. "Are you okay?"

When my son finds me in the café forty-five minutes later, he's reluctant to upset me further by describing what he saw inside the Documentation Centre. After coffee he says, "Why is there so much hatred in the world? I just don't get it."

"Let's see the DP camp where Bubbie was. Maybe you'll have your faith restored." I touch his arm. "What happened in many of the DP camps after the war is the opposite of what happened in the Nazi concentration camps."

At the Bergen-Belsen Displaced Persons camp, only a couple of kilometres away, we learn that the DP camp was a Nazi military training base during the 1930s. After the British liberated the Bergen-Belsen concentration camp in 1945, they set up an emergency hospital at the former Nazi military base to care for survivors suffering from typhus and extreme malnutrition. Thirteen thousand former concentration camp prisoners, too ill to recover, died after liberation. A short time later the British transformed the emergency hospital and military base into a facility for displaced people. I tell Simon that Mamaleh, pretending to be the daughter of an older couple, travelled from Poland to restart her life right here.

Simon and I are allowed to enter only one of the barracks that housed displaced persons, M.B. 89, now repurposed as the Learning Center. Mamaleh might have walked these halls as a teenager, though it's hard to picture her in such a sterile place. I nudge Simon with my elbow. "Can you believe that your grandmother lived here as a lonely kid on forged papers with fake parents?"

"Not really," he says. "Maybe Bubbie was safer in a DP camp in Germany than in Poland after the war, but what kind of life was this?"

"Good enough for her to make a comeback. What choice did she have? Out of necessity she made it work—rose from the ashes, you could say—on the very soil where the Nazis had trained soldiers to pursue an aggressive, hateful war. C'mon, Simon. How stunning is that?"

We're exhausted, but I insist that we make the one-kilometre trek to the Glyn-Hughes Hospital before dark. Once a hospital serving the Nazi armed forces, it became a state-of-the-art medical facility after liberation, treating survivors and delivering babies. A cornucopia of babies. I was one of thousands of infants born in the maternity ward here. My throat tightens as we approach the sprawling, two-storey building that gave me life.

Standing in front of the locked hospital gates, I am caught between a sob and a laugh. Mamaleh's writing tablet is pressed to my chest. In my purse I carry my authentic birth certificate issued by this very hospital. I've reread the faded document many times: "Hinda Schreiber. Date of birth: February 16, 1949. Father: Herman Petersen. Mother: Shayna Schreiber."

Should I count my birth father, Herman Petersen, as a member of my family although I didn't know him? Should I add Petersen to my name? As an intern on the tuberculosis ward in the hospital, he likely played a significant role in Mamaleh's recovery from the disease. I suspect that her affair with him also lifted her depleted spirits. I now realize that my stepfather, Hal, was trying to tell me something when he used to say everybody in your family counts, no matter when or how the person enters your life or exits from it. Blood is stronger than water.

I remove my birth certificate from my purse and slip it into my shoe. My toes wiggle over its smooth surface in the way Mamaleh caressed her absent family when she needed them the most. I feel a jolt of energy flow from her to me, as if she and my birth father are present with us at the hospital gate.

But, the truth is, without Irene's intervention, I would never have put the pieces of my mother's story together. Mamaleh told Irene that she and Hal obtained a forged birth certificate for me before they left

Germany for Canada. The new birth certificate listed my father as Haskel Alinsky, my mother's husband, to save me from the humiliation and shame of illegitimacy. I suspect that Mamaleh was no stranger to illegitimacy herself.

I edge closer to Simon. "You know, my mother made me promise to give Irene her house on Maple Drive."

"And? You're telling me this now because…"

"I'm telling you because Mamaleh can only rest in peace if she knows that her wish for Irene Santos to inherit her house has been granted."

Simon gives me a quizzical look. "In your entire life you never listened to your mother," he says. "Why now?"

"That's easy. Irene has given me the gift of truth. Without the trust my mother placed in her, I might never have known who my father was. Don't worry. I'll find a different house for you and your family, your own house, as it should be."

"If you say so," he says. "Suddenly you're changing all the rules. Who knew?"

Simon and I walk back to the Learning Center from the hospital gate, tracing the steps my mother must have made on many occasions. I listen to the sounds of the spruce forest on either side of the road and forget to remember the atrocities that happened in those days gone by. As we walk, I take Simon's hand and bury our entwined fingers in the pocket of his jacket.

"Do you know who T.S. Eliot was?" I ask him.

"Um. He was some sort of political bigwig, right?"

"Not quite. He was a poet. Being here reminds me of the lines from one of his poems."

"Okay. Let's hear it."

"'Last year's words belong to last year's language. And next year's words await another voice.'"

"Cool, but I'm not sure what it means. Is there more?"

"I think Eliot was saying that an ending can sometimes be a beginning. It reminds me of that painted metal rooster in a front garden on Maple Drive. Roosters usher in a new day—a fresh start— with their shrill scream."

"Obviously." Simon shrugs.

Okay. I've failed to impress my son with the wisdom of T.S. Eliot's poem, "Little Gidding." The message in the rooster's crow also fell flat. But somewhere in the clouds when we're flying from Frankfurt to Toronto, I drop my head on his shoulder, satisfied that our journey provided the closure I needed and the opening required to move forward.

CHAPTER 41

Jonathan

May 2024

Excuse me for being royally pissed off with the constant roadwork that makes travelling from A to B in this city almost impossible, particularly on my bike. Road closures, detours, and restrictions screw up the arterial roads and side streets. For fuck's sake, with the traffic jammed everywhere I turn, it'll take me more than thirty minutes to get from the club to the restaurant where those crazed pickleball fanatics are meeting for lunch today. But hey, green split-pea soup is always on the menu, and for that I'm making a special effort to attend the gathering. Best pea soup in the city. Everyone knows that. And I'd like to see Heidi. I'm sure she'll be there with her peeps. She never misses a party with the pickleball gang. Oops. Almost had a collision at the intersection of Wilson and Bathurst with a driver making a right turn. I bet the jerk was on his phone. Who isn't distracted these days?

Here's the thing. I've had the time to rethink my relationship with Heidi since Sylvia died. That change of heart began, oddly enough, with a rotator cuff injury. I suspect that my shoulder joint had been deteriorating over a long period of time. Obviously, in my line of work, overuse injuries are common. But after the loss of Sylvia, I upped my participation in highly competitive pickleball tournaments. Otherwise, the unbearable grief over her death was going to destroy me. So, without much forethought and in a flurry of enthusiasm, I decided to attend a big pickleball tournament in Tampa, Florida. I figured that training for the event and travelling south would be a great tonic. Just the boost I needed. After all, it's considered one of the coolest pickleball parties on the planet. Having registered and purchased weather refund insurance, I was ready to go. I even found a partner from the Players Needing a Partner list. But becoming a pickleball champ in Tampa was not in the cards for me. In our first game I heard a popping in my shoulder. A few minutes later I felt a rip, followed by shoulder pain that was so intense I had to forfeit the game. Regrettably, the registration fee wasn't covered by insurance. My shoulder felt so weak that I could barely lift the paddle.

Back in Toronto my physiotherapist reminded me that the recovery time on rotator cuff injuries can be very long. We're talking months, and sometimes more than a year! I didn't need a PhD in psychology to realize that a career shift would be a wise move. But what was I qualified to do? I wanted to remain in the fitness field, but not necessarily in the competitive or even recreational sports area. Been there, done that. I felt ready to take on something new, something slow and meditative rather than fast and hard-hitting. Long story short, I'm retraining as a therapeutic yoga instructor. Yup. Hard to believe for a macho guy like me. Yet I'm finding that it's not a bad fit.

One of the unintended consequences of my career shift is a new appreciation of someone I'm sorry to say I've always undervalued— Heidi. The meditative piece of the therapeutic yoga training got me thinking about the relationship I've had not only with her, but with other women, some satisfactory and most unsatisfactory. One day, lying on my yoga mat in corpse pose, it occurred to me that I could have done better by Heidi. I misjudged her from the outset, and I'm man enough to admit it. I've always put her squarely in the pickleball box, but the longer I know her, the more I see that the pickleball slot doesn't entirely do her justice. I mean, sure it's impressive that she's so keen on playing pickleball in her seventies. Heidi's real age is seventy-five. She confessed that her actual year of her birth was 1949, not 1950, as was stated on her forged, second birth certificate. At seventy-five, she could easily be an old fuddy duddy sitting at home, talking to her cats. (Not cats. I forgot. She's allergic to them.) Instead, Heidi throws herself into every game. Each whack of the pickleball is an assertion that she's worth something, which, in my books, makes her a winner. She's adamant that her life retain its value. And she's not done yet. Don't ever try to use Heidi's age to discredit her. You'll regret it because she'll chew you out, like she did me.

"Hey. Learn how to drive, you fucking bully." The Subaru that just passed me was much too close. If I fall off the bike and reinjure my shoulder, I'm toast.

Okay. Never mind that. Back to Heidi. The way I see her now is like this: She was born into a silent generation of women. Women in her cohort were taught to keep their chins up and not complain. I see this kind of behaviour all the time at the club. Older women don't want to make a scene. If something goes wrong on the courts or in the change room, they want to be the sort of person who would dust herself off, put on lipstick, and move on.

Heidi defies that mindset. She has the chutzpah not to fall into the ageist trap. When she plays pickleball, it's about much more than winning that particular game. She's making a claim that a woman in her seventies still has active years ahead of her—physically, socially, mentally. I respect that. I'm willing to bet that she'll be the same at eighty, if she only stops self-sabotaging.

That's where my new interest in therapeutic yoga kicks in. We're working on our self-sabotaging habits, hers and mine, by taking a step back, going for walks, doing yoga, and getting away from the hustle of the city and the frenzy of the courts. Rest days, we call them, though I'm more committed to the life of a yogi than she is. I love my sun salutations, and she loves her pickleball.

Okay. I've made it here in one piece. Heidi saved a seat for me. There must be forty picklers at this banquet table. I sit down next to her and press my hands together, fingers touching and pointing up. "Namaste," I greet her.

"Hello, Jonathan. Glad to see you." She gives me a sideways glance, then smiles. It seems to be a peaceful smile or maybe it's a shy smile. Heidi, shy? No freaking way.

CHAPTER 42

Heidi

June 2024

By the time late spring arrives in Toronto, I've splurged on a highly rated Joola paddle and bought two-toned outdoor training pickleballs to work on my topspin. The online scheduler is buzzing with people scrambling to find games. The courts on Maple Drive are busier than ever. As soon as I see a suitable game posted, I grab the last slot:

Lisa Melman has organized a new Doubles session at Maple Drive Park on Tuesday, June 4 from 7:00 PM to 9:00 PM.

Like magic, our pickleball crowd coalesces for the spring/summer season of outdoor play. Lisa and Joanne returned about two months ago from pickleball paradise in Florida. Fuck. They have a huge advantage over the rest of us who played indoors throughout the frigid months. They know how to compensate for wind and sun. They've had access to more court time and stiffer competition in leagues. And they discovered pickleball long before it became popular up north.

Hell, as snowbirds, Lisa and Joanne have been playing pickleball for years. No fair. Damn. Before I've gotten off the bench, before I've walked onto the court and lifted my paddle, the chatter in my head threatens to grind my focus into fine particles of sawdust.

But standing at the baseline, ready to serve, I visualize the diagonal trajectory of the ball going exactly where I want it to go. While taking a few deep breaths, I assure myself that I'm a decent player. I can do this. I nod at my partner, Ron, who gives me the go-ahead. Throughout the game we play at the kitchen line, where the exchange of shots is so rapid that there's no time to think, judge, worry, fear, regret, or blame. My eyes are pinned on the action of the ball and the movement of the players. It's an almost childlike feeling, free of apologies and self-congratulation, to achieve that fine balance between humility and arrogance that will win the game.

As I walk off the court, I wonder how I arrived at this place and this game at my advanced age. Nothing in my history predetermined my arrival here. I can't attribute my pickleball obsession to previous athletic experience, a driving competitive instinct, a strong body, or the mental toughness of an athlete. In fact, Mamaleh discouraged my involvement in sports, which she considered dangerous and unladylike behaviour. Maybe my athletic birth father is looking down on me with pride, but I doubt he knew of my existence, and I've made no effort to trace him. It's not about him. It's about me.

Only Sylvia is missing from our pickleball reunion. More than six months after her death, we have no explanation of how she died, and we will likely never discover the real cause of her demise. In an impromptu meeting on the court after the game, we exchange ideas for how to honour her life. We've done nothing to celebrate her yet. Can someone write a song for her, I ask. I'm not sure if Sylvia would prefer an anthem, a ballad, or a lullaby. Maybe we should have a potluck lunch to reminisce about our time together or raise money for a charitable donation in her name. Other ideas? We could pay tribute to Sylvia by dedicating a bench in the park to her, someone suggests. And we could add an inscription that reads: *Sylvia Greene. Always in our hearts. In 2 Win.* I'm in favour of that. In the end, we opt for a march from her house to the courts on Maple Drive, using social media to invite pickleball players who knew Sylvia or even those who didn't, to join in commemorating her and saluting the game that almost saved her. If only I could rewind time to those early matches when Sylvia seemed so innocent, with that blue metal headband holding back her streaked hair, and the summer sun animated the courts on Maple Drive.

Late on a gusty afternoon in June, about thirty people in our network meet at Sylvia's house to begin our march to the park on Maple Drive. We are paddle-wielding warriors, swallowing tears Sylvia would not want us to shed for her. Jonathan walks beside me and brushes his fingers against mine as we cross the few streets to our destination. When we arrive at the courts, my anger erupts. I kick away a few pebbles and grit my teeth. How cruel and unfair her death was. After we form a semicircle, I step forward, face flushed, to deliver a eulogy for her.

"Dear friends: We gather today to mourn the loss of our beloved pickleball mate, Sylvia Greene, and to celebrate her life. Let me tell you that hundreds of years ago, in June of 1789, defiant representatives of the nonprivileged classes in France gathered on a tennis court outside of Paris and took an oath to never separate until a written constitution for France had been established. The Tennis Court Oath was a revolutionary document asserting that authority derives from the people and their representatives. It defined the fundamental values of liberty and equality.

"So too we are gathered here today, old and young, in solidarity to affirm our collective commitment to end any form of abuse on or off the pickleball court. We join forces to oppose all expressions of sexism and ageism, whether in sport or life. But, above all, today we lift our paddles to honour the memory of our pickleball colleague Sylvia Greene, who loved the game and the comradery she felt when she was among us.

"I hereby declare an annual tournament in Sylvia's name: The Sylvia Greene Annual Pickleball Tournament. As Sylvia often said, there is no need to be fanatical about pickleball. We are more than the game, more than our obsession to play. Through pickleball we care for each other. We are part of a community, a found family. We belong."

I step back, return to the perimeter of our semicircle, and point to a mound of dirt just outside of the chain-link fence, close to the bench where we found Sylvia's blue hairband almost a year ago. A few of us dug a hole and buried her hairband there a couple of days before our march today.

"Let the courts on Maple Drive be Sylvia's burial ground," I say. "Rest in peace, dearest friend."

I scan the faces of so many people who were once unfamiliar and who are now kin. The sun shines over the pickleball courts, casting a golden hue on the freshly painted lines. The rhythmic sound of paddles striking the lightweight plastic balls fills the air, accompanied by laughter, shouts of triumph, and occasional groans of defeat. On the far court a competition is just beginning. I hear the first server announce the starting score: 0-0-2. Those numbers feel like the prelude to a great drama about to unfold. We are seasoned actors performing on a small rectangular stage. And the title of our smash hit is *Pickleball*. You must be kidding, a spectator might be tempted to say. Is that name a joke, or what?

The End

Acknowledgements

The Courts on Maple Drive begins with a pickleball game. In the novel, a group of players comes together to engage in an activity that is meaningful and special for them. The same could be said for creating a book. Although writing a novel often begins as a solitary activity, the truth is many people are involved in the experience of bringing a work of fiction into the world.

I am extremely fortunate to have worked with the outstanding editor Marie-Lynn Hammond on this novel. Her exceptional editorial skills and wisdom strengthened the manuscript in numerous ways. To her long list of achievements, she can rightfully add book midwife. I am grateful to Greg Ioannou and Cheryl Hawley at Iguana Books for their commitment to making this book the best it can be. They brought a clear and collaborative approach to the publishing process.

I am blessed to be surrounded by a sensational group of pickleball players who are steady morale boosters and enthusiastic champions of my work. I thank all of them for the many hours of playtime we've spent together and for the creation of a compassionate community of people who care for each other. I appreciate the excellent feedback I received from early readers of this novel, namely Lois Eisen, Desre Kramer, and Erin Paterson. Elizabeth Drucker Spivak kindly took the promotional photograph of me.

Above all, I'm indebted to my family, particularly my husband, Myer Siemiatycki, who graciously took over on the home front while I either locked myself away to write or escaped to play pickleball.

Myer's enormous support made the book possible. His way with words in English and Yiddish is always helpful. My sister-in-law Debbie Siemiatycki and her husband, Avi Slodovnik, are a continuous source of encouragement, as are my cherished cousins Sondra Baron and Sally Zimmerman. My sons, Matti and Elliot, my daughters-in-law, Kristin Olson and Asha Forrester, and my six grandchildren motivate me with their joyful mix of love and laughter. I dedicate this novel to my late brother, Les Benick, whose exuberant participation in the St. Louis, Missouri, handball community was legendary. My brother's voice continues to inspire me every time I step onto a pickleball court.